THE
SHARP
EMPIRE III

TYLER JOHNS

Order this book online at www.trafford.com
or email orders@trafford.com

Most Trafford titles are also available at major online book retailers.

Printed in the United States of America.

ISBN: 978-1-4907-1287-1 (sc)
ISBN: 978-1-4907-1286-4 (e)

Trafford rev. 09/06/2013

 www.trafford.com

North America & international
toll-free: 1 888 232 4444 (USA & Canada)
fax: 812 355 4082

CHAPTERS

FOREWORD

The Sharp Empire has been a cruel diabolical evil force, especially to humanity and nature of its own kind. The emperor, Hieronymus Sharp, a hybrid of a green lizard and a cobra, was formed to create evil immortal monsters and to revive prehistoric beasts of his own for his forces.

A team of freedom fighters headed by Nala Boomer, a lioness, was sent to investigate the empire's plans. She was betrayed by a dragon named, Dermazzo Joustiáño, who became the Serpential count. Boomer was executed with the machine called the Spruce Noose that was used to hang her.

Later, Emperor Sharp had assassinated many leaders whom he won every war against. The Serpentials had kidnapped a young Irish princess named, Mariana Izodorro. Heavenly Federal pilots rescued her and made her lead them into war as several years passed. The princess commanded several spies to steal the plans from the Sharp Empire's biosphere, the Death Scale. The Serpentials captured the princess and created new plans.

A new team of freedom fighters including Skinamarinky-Dinky-Dink Skinamarinky-Doo (an orangutan), Zinger Warsp (an old giant wasp), and the Invisi-Bot (a human-like robot programmed to turn invisible), the three who were with Nala Boomer, came to be. The new freedom fighters called forth were Captain Tiblo Tigro (a tiger), Manda Monka (an alien wolf), Shana Cargon (a kangaroo), Martino Izodorro (the princess's older brother), and Regulto Beauxon (a human scientist with a medicine to transform into a beast named Rufus). As they were sent to investigate the Death Scale, the Serpentials executed the princess by drowning her in Lake Prisoner where she was weighed down and frozen into a crystal. She was lifted into the air by robots, powered up with the emperor's finger lightning. They created a satellite.

After the execution, the freedom fighters had a battle with many of the emperor's henchmonsters. After those battles, they were confronted by the white condor god, Artidector. He said that he and his children would bring the princess back to life.

And so, the freedom fighters escaped the Death Scale. They flew with their large ship, the Great Red Shark. They fought their way to their base in the Orion Nebula. The Death Scale moved toward that base and the freedom fighters defended it by blowing up the Death Scale in four major pieces. That was just the beginning of the war, but so it went on.

A year later, the Heaven Federation hid in an underwater base on a newborn ice planet. The Serpentials claimed to eliminate the Federation, but they escaped. The freedom fighters were given a quest to find the hidden artifacts called, gem scales, which were known to hold the Death Scale together. As the scales were collected, the Death Scale started to get back together again.

The freedom fighters were later confronted by Count Joustiáño, who they remembered denied and betrayed Nala Boomer. They fought against him for the memory with their wasp friend, Zinger, who told the truth about all that happened.

Now, it is time for another mission . . . .

CHAPTER 1

ASTEROID COMBAT

There is a great complication for the heroes. The gem
scales were used to bring the Death Scale back together.
The freedom fighters must find the last gem scale in
the city of Gutville, a disgusting town of disembodied
digestive organs.
A new enemy is about to arise in the distance of space
and the freedom fighters are to continue their destiny . . .

Soaring through space in their ships, the Heavenly
Federal freedom fighters entered a field of asteroids on
their way to find the last gem scale on the southwestern
quarter of the Death Scale. There lay the gruesome dead
organ-filled city of Gutville. On their way through the field
were space mines.

"Enemy mines ahead!" Manda Monka was the first to speak.

"Shoot them down from being marked!" Captain Tiblo Tigro commanded. The freedom fighters used their ships' laser guns to destroy the mines in their path. Martino Izodorro zoomed around destroying multiple mines.

"Come on!" he said as a nearby mine beeped. "Whoa!" Martino flew away as the mine exploded.

"Be careful!" said Tiblo. "They explode when you get to close!"

Regulto Beauxon flew around mines shooting the ones that blinked.

"God, I hate this," he said as he shot the mines one by one. A few more exploded. A beam damaged the ships. Soon they were clear from the mines.

"That was a close call!" said Shana Cargon.

"Let's hit the road!" said Tiblo. They all flew away from the asteroid field and there came some enemy fighter ships.

"Enemy fighters ahead!" said Skinamarinky-Dinky-Dink Skinamarinky-Doo. "We've got company!"

"This is where the fun begins!" said Tiblo. The freedom fighters started firing at the ships one by one.

"I have this one," said Manda as she shot down ships and barrel-rolled, flicking off enemy shots. Shana tried shooting one enemy down and Martino finished it.

"Hey! He was mine!" Shana shouted.

"Well, excuse me!" said Martino.

"Stand by!" Tiblo commanded. "I'm about to launch a bomb!" He opened up a hatch at the bottom of his ship and flew above the enemy ships, dropping the bomb. Then it exploded with a white blast.

"Enemies eliminated!" said Tiblo.

"Finally," said Skinamar.

"The place we're looking for is right there," said Martino, as he found the southwestern quarter of the Death Scale in his sight.

"Good eye," said Tiblo. "Let's go, scouts!" The freedom fighters flew down to where Martino found the disgusting town of Gutville on radar on the quarter. They landed nearby piles of dead intestines from prehistoric beasts that roamed the Death Scale before the system lost its star.

"Oh, gross!" said Shana as she got out of her Wallaby Wing ship.

"This place is moldy rotten and I . . . can't . . . <cough!> . . . breathe!" said Regulto, as he fell to the muddy ground of slime.

Tiblo grabbed gas masks from his emergency pack inside his Tiger Shark ship. "We have gas masks!" he said as he put one on.

"I've got some!" said Skinamar as he put one on from his ship, the Ape Smacker.

Tiblo gave masks to his other scouts: Martino, then Shana, Regulto, and Manda.

"Now it's easier to breathe," said Manda putting on the mask she received.

"This place looks deserted," said Martino.

"Not quite," said Tiblo. "There are some slime balls still hiding around here."

Suddenly, a slug with a pod of oversized maggots came out of hiding. He found the freedom fighters standing in one place.

"You are intruders!" said the slug.

"Well, excuse us," said Martino. "We are only trying to visit someone."

"You can visit our king," said the slug. "Follow us." The freedom fighters followed the slug and the maggots to a bio-dome in the middle of the town where a monstrous king ruled over the nasty town.

"I have a bad feeling about all this," said Shana.

"Where is Zinger when you need him?" said Skinamar.

Inside the bio-dome, the slug led the heroes straight through the hall into the center room where the throne room was.

CHAPTER 2

A FAVOR FOR A GUTVILLAIN

Inside the throne room was large, soft stool. There sat the king, a large, soda can-shaped bodied monster with a hard head with zigzag toothed jaws, six tentacles and a spiny dragon's tail. He wore a red crown with a golden octopus head on top with its tentacles dividing the crown's segments. He held a scepter, within his tentacles, with a brass shaft and a blue orb head topped with another gold octopus.

As the slug led the freedom fighters in the room, he said, "Your majesty, you have visitors."

"Awe!" said the king. "Introduce yourselves."

"I'm Captain Tiblo Tigro," said Tiblo, "and these are my freedom fighting scouts of the Heaven Federation."

"Martino Izodorro," said Martino.

"Skinamarinky-Dinky-Dink Skinamarinky-Doo," said Skinamar.

"Shana Cargon," said Shana.

"Manda Monka," said Manda.

"Regulto Beauxon," said Regulto.

"Heaven Federation?" said the king. "You are enemies to our great emperor. I am King Drinx-For-a-Gut."

"Drinx?" asked some of the heroes.

"A substance that seems alien to you," said the king, "but it is a dew-like substance in my digestive system." Next to him sat an ant-like figure with a long, bird-like beak and two lizard-like tails.

"This is my right-hand servant, Tropical Gut," said the king.

"Greetings!" said Tropical Gut. "What is your purpose here?"

"We are here looking for a gem scale," said Tiblo, "the last one on our list."

King Drinx-For-a-Gut started laughing. He laughed and so did all the slime-oozing invertebrates in the room. It went on and on until the king said his message, "The scales are to be protected. Putting them in their rightful places brings this biosphere back together."

"We know," said Martino. "We've done it before."

"This scale is guarded by the emperor's largest monster, the Gore King," said King Drinx-For-a-Gut. "He is hidden in the Gore Caverns, which should be west of this town. Now you may go. Release them!" He commanded the slug.

The freedom fighters went ahead through another hallway in the dome. There were scientific labs with containers of slimy invertebrates being tested in genetics.

"There's nothing here but a bunch of mollusks and leeches," said Shana.

"The caverns are the next part of our quest," said Tiblo.

"We should get there without problems," said Martino. The freedom fighters put on their gas masks for the outside town.

"It's always as smelly as heck around here," said Skinamar. They all walked through the back of the town. Back inside the dome, a snail burned a bolt in a fireplace. The king picked it up with grabbers. He placed it in his mouth and steam flowed through his gills. He coughed it out like an owl pellet.

Soon the freedom fighters were out of Gutville and on a grassy plain. They took off their gas masks and put them in their packs. They were on their way to the Gore Caverns.

CHAPTER 3

THE GORE CAVERNS

The caverns were built up of brown geode rocks. The inside was rather dark. There lived many creatures of hostility inside the holes in the walls.

"This place gives me the heebie-jeebies," said Skinamar.

"I hear centipedes crawling around," said Martino. He looked in a hole and a centipede-like creature jumped out fast.

"Whoa!" Martino jumped back.

"Careful!" said Tiblo. "These crawlers are poisonous."

A spider-like creature crawled on the ceiling and dropped to the floor. It hissed and shot webs from its spinneret at the freedom fighters. They dodged them. Tiblo shot his twin blasters at the creature repeatedly until he killed it. The freedom fighters ran down the paths away from the crawlers and followed the road until they reached a large cavern. It was about on fifth of a mile wide, enough room for one monster to move around. The only thing standing inside was a large monster statue ahead in the dark.

"YOU THERE!" Manda shouted through the cavern. The echo repeated her voice.

"Here let me try," said Skinamar coming to the front of the team. "I'm a professional at communicating with echoes." He put his hands around his mouth and started shouting, "HELLO!" The echo repeated it. Skinamar then called out, "HOW ARE YOU?!" The echo repeated that quote. "I'M FINE HOW ABOUT *YOU?!*" Skinamar shouted to the echo again. It repeated that quote, too. "DUDE, YOU'RE SAYING THE EXACT SAME STUFF THAT *I'M* SAYING!" Skinamar said. The echo repeated that next quote. "I've got it," said Skinamar to the freedom fighters. He inhaled some air and shouted, "I'M AN IDIOT!" The echo repeated it. Then he said, "YOU'RE AN IDIOT!" The echo repeated that, too. Skinamar moved his eyes around and said, "Well anyway, the coast is clear. Let's get down." The freedom fighters went down to lower ground.

"That statue must be the monster we're after," said Shana.

"I don't know," said Regulto. "It's a tall statue."

They all went forth for a closer look at the statue. Martino felt its foot.

"It's all solid," he said, knocking on the toe claw.

"Something's shining up there," said Manda as she looked up at a shine of a little light. "That must be the scale."

"I've got it!" said Skinamar. "My sunray phaser should do the job."

"Skinamar, no!" said Martino. "That's a bad idea."

"You're gonna have to trust me on this," said Skinamar. He shot his sun ray phaser at the statue. It burned a large hot spot; something bad was about to occur.

CHAPTER 4

THE GORE KING

All of a sudden, the monster was about to awaken. An earthquake was made. The statue crumbled and rocks broke off of it.

"It's the Gore King!" cried Shana.

"He's got the Gem Scale!" shouted Regulto.

"He was under stone sleep and now we woke him up!" said Tiblo.

Rocks fell off the monster's four legs, front belly, four arms, and face. The one eye opened with two yellow slits. It had a pair of curled, ram-like horns, a long tail with a bulb of unknown organs and a stinger for paralyzing its enemies; and its claws were dark blue. It had a group of ten chelicerae surrounding its mouth with blue fangs. It held a crystal white gem scale (the one the heroes searched for). As it broke out of its sleep as a statue, the rocks fell off and the monster tossed the scale in the air and caught it in its chelicerae. It swallowed it and exhaled.

"Oh no!" said Martino. "He swallowed it! What do we do?!"

"We're too late!" said Manda.

"Take cover!" commanded Tiblo. "I'll handle this beast!" He pulled out his blasters and started shooting. The Gore King screeched out. The freedom fighters hid behind rocks as Tiblo started attacking the monster face to face. Shana tried attacking it behind. She had a new weapon, a blue hyper-powered boomerang, which she threw at the monster's tail bulb. The tail fell and the monster stung her. Shana was paralyzed by the venom inside the bulb that flowed through the stinger.

"Shana!" Tiblo shouted. He shot the tail bulb repeatedly and jumped on the monster's back. Skinamar dragged Shana to a safe place behind a rock. Tiblo jumped to the Gore King's face and the monster caught him in its chelicerae. It swallowed him up.

"Tiblo!" shouted Martino. The Gore King screeched out. Inside its stomach, Tiblo fell into its gooey digestive acid. He got back up on his hind paws protected with boots. A pendulum attached to the stomach's ceiling appeared with the gem scale inside. Tiblo shot at it to loosen the pendulum's stem. After many shots, the Gore King had hernia and Tiblo was taken back up to the mouth. The monster hurled him out.

"Are you alright?" asked Manda as she approached Tiblo covered in slime.

"Watch out!" Tiblo shouted. The Gore King started slamming its head at the ground by Tiblo. He and Manda rolled away to dodge it. It lifted its head and shot a glob of slime from its mouth. Martino confronted the monster and aimed at its throat with his digital disk launcher. He shot a homing disk that flew around the monster's neck and hit it at the front of its throat. Soon it was his turn to be eaten. The Gore King bent down and grabbed Martino within its chelicerae.

"MARTY!" shouted Skinamar.

"That's the same thing that just happened to me," said Tiblo.

The Gore King swallowed Martino. He followed the same path that Tiblo followed inside the monster's stomach. He fell in the acid and got up. He saw the gem scale in the pendulum.

"Tiblo's been in here alright," he said. He shot the pendulum's stem with his disk launcher. He walked to it and grabbed the sticky head trying to reach the scale. The pendulum tore down to the floor. Martino walked back to the Gore King's esophagus. The monster started to upchuck. Martino was hurled out of the monster's stomach along with the gem scale next to him, dried up with slime.

"Marty's alive!" said Skinamar. Regulto was dragging Shana, who was still paralyzed, out of the cavern. The Gore King wiggled its head. As the freedom fighters escaped, the Gore King leaned back and slammed its head on the ground. It started to feel faint from hernia. Shana was about to awaken from the paralyzing sting.

CHAPTER 5

THE LAST GEM SCALE

"We did it!" said Skinamar. "We got the last gem scale!"

"What's . . . going on?" said Shana as she barely awoke from the paralyzing sting. "I couldn't move for a while and we're out of the cave."

"You were paralyzed by that big monster," said Skinamar.

"At least we defeated it," said Manda.

"We got to get this scale back to where it belongs," said Martino. The freedom fighters walked out the Gore Caverns. They were on their way back to Gutville. As they got there, they put on their gas masks. They walked back inside the bio-dome and met back up with King Drinx-For-a-Gut.

"Your majesty," said Tiblo. "We have the scale."

"Here it is," said Martino as he held up the gem scale. "You want it? Go get it!" He threw the scale by the doors.

"No!" shouted King Drinx-For-a-Gut. "Foolish freedom fighters! You'll pay for this insubordination!" He used his scepter to create a magic beam and slammed it on the ground to form a quake, knocking the heroes down. "Gutvillains, attack!" the king commanded.

Slugs, squid, maggots, worms, and other invertebrates used their warfare against the freedom fighters as they ran around the throne room. Martino grabbed the gem scale on the rush.

"What a stupid idea you made, Marty!" said Tiblo.

"Grab the gem scale!" the king commanded. "Secure the heroes!" Gutvillains scrambled all over the place. They chased after the freedom fighters.

As the fight went on, the king pressed a secret button on the arm of his throne. A hatch opened on the floor below. Inside was a rocket. It rose up to the floor. The king called for the gem scale. A slug grabbed it from Martino and brought it to the king. Tiblo followed him and leaped aboard the rocket. The king started the rocket with a lever that activated its engine. It started burning the underground. Martino jumped at the side ladder. The rocket blasted up to the bio-dome's ceiling and broke a hole through the roof. Inside the rocket, Tiblo confronted the king, taking off his gas mask, and said, "You'll never get away with this, your royal sliminess!"

"The gem scale is mine!" said King Drinx-For-a-Gut. "You are my prisoner, Captain Tigro." He let slime pour out of his glands from his tentacles and splattered it on Tiblo's arms against the rocket's wall. It stuck him there.

Outside, Martino climbed the ladder as the rocket reached for space. He could barely breathe. He reached in his pack for something. He found a laser-bladed knife. He lit it and cut a crack in the rocket's roof. He punched it down inside and it fell on the king's head while he was activating the satellite mode. The engines stopped burning. Martino jumped inside. He took off his gas mask.

"Surprise, your grossness!" he said.

"Marty!" said Tiblo.

"I'm taking this scale back to where it belongs, now!" said King Drinx-For-a-Gut as he grabbed a parachute pack and jumped out of the rocket preparing to sky dive.

"Marty!" said Tiblo. "Get me out of this slime!" Martino went to him and used his laser knife to cut the slime and set Tiblo free. They both went up at the rocket's side doors. The king's parachute opened up.

"When I give the signal," said Tiblo as he and Martino pressed their feet against the doors, "we kick these doors down." He and Martino turned their boots on "magnet mode" lifting one foot up. Tiblo turned on a bomb and set it on the rocket's floor.

"A bomb?!" Martino asked.

"Ready," said Tiblo. "NOW!" They both kicked the doors and fell outside, chasing after King Drinx-For-a-Gut. As they did, the bomb beeped faster and exploded, destroying the rocket.

"No!" said the king as Tiblo and Martino chased after the octopus head-shaped parachute. They were using the doors as skydiving surfboards. Back on the ground, the rest of the crew could barely see the skydiving ruckus.

"I'll see what they're up to," said Skinamar as he brought a helium tank from his pack. He put the tank's tube in his mouth, inflating himself into a balloon. After inhaling the helium, he floated up to the sky to see what Tiblo and Martino were up to. Martino was grabbing onto the king's parachute and performing a stunt. He did flips and twirls with the door he was on.

"WHOO-HOOOOO!" he shouted. He fell down toward the quarter's ground along with Tiblo. Skinamar exhaled the helium slowly and fell back down to the others. Tiblo crashed into a palm tree near the edge of the quarter and fell off the door he rode on. He broke his back.

"Ow!" he shouted.

"Tiblo!" Martino called out as he landed on solid ground. He turned off the magnet mode on his boots and went off his ridden door and ran toward Tiblo.

"So long, freedom fighters!" called King-Drinx-For-a-Gut. "I've got the scale! I'm taking it to its place!" He soared down toward his hometown to put the gem scale in its rightful place.

A moment passed. Artidector appeared with the freedom fighters' ships.

CHAPTER 6

ESCAPE FROM THE RECONSTRUCTION

"Artidector!" said Skinamar, with a helium affected voice.

"You're back in time," said Shana.

"Our ships are out of that dump," said Regulto.

"About time you showed up to help us leave," said Manda.

"The last gem scale has been recovered," said Artidector. "I have moved your ships here so you will leave more easily. Now we must leave." The freedom fighters headed for their ships, all except Martino, sitting by Tiblo aching.

"Come, Martino," Artidector spoke to him as Martino tried to drag Tiblo to somewhere safe. "Leave him," Artidector said. "The Death Scale will soon be together again. You must let him heal."

Martino stood up and said, "He might heal faster if we call a hospital ship."

"Martino," said Artidector, "there is no time. Come before it is too late."

"Come on, Marty!" Skinamar called out as the helium in his voice wore out. "The Great Red Shark is waiting for us in space."

"Go on without me, Marty," said Tiblo as he tried to get up with a broken back. Martino went ahead with the others.

"Let's get going!" said Shana. "We're running out of time!"

"Board your ships," said Artidector. The freedom fighters got into their cockpits.

"What about Tiblo?" Martino asked.

"He will be just fine," said Artidector. He used a blessing on Tiblo to heal his spine and ribs together. Tiblo still rested until he was finally able to get up.

As the freedom fighters flew away, Martino witnessed the rest of the Death Scale just a few miles away. It slowly drew closer with the southwestern quarter as it moved toward the biosphere. Tiblo was up and able to move again. He ran to his ship remaining on the quarter. He boarded it to catch up with the others. As the other five freedom fighters headed for the Great Red Shark, that ship was hovering and slowly moving toward their position opening the docking bay. They boarded the Shark and went up the stairs to the top deck to meet up with Zinger Warsp and the Invisi-Bot.

"Mission accomplished, Zinger!" said Martino.

"You're back," said Zinger. "Hopefully you've recovered the last gem scale. Where is your captain?"

"He's still behind," said Martino. "He has a problem with his back."

"Well, I suppose he should be healing by now," said the Invisi-Bot.

Suddenly, in front of the Great Red Shark appeared a red-orange ship with stripes.

"There he is," said Martino as he witnessed the ship.

"Tiger Shark to Great Red Shark," it was Tiblo's voice. "Standing by for clearance." He entered the Shark's docking bay.

"About time he got better," said Martino.

"About time he came back," said Manda.

"About time he showed up," said Shana.

"Finally," said Skinamar. Tiblo walked all the way up with the others to rejoin them.

"I feel better now," said Tiblo.

"The Great Red Shark is ready to leave," said the Invisi-Bot.

"Let's head home," said Tiblo as he walked forward to the dashboard. He sat in the pilot's cockpit and activated the Great Red Shark's engines. He flew the ship and activated the hyper-drive. The ship disappeared in distant space.

A minute later, the ship arrived by a station where the Heavenly Federal forces were working in. Tiblo turned off the hyper-drive and landed the ship in a hangar bay nearby. As the freedom fighters walked off, Tiblo received a call from General Gando Grizzle.

"General Grizzle here," he said as his hologram appeared in Tiblo's wrist communicator. "How was your mission, Captain?"

"We recovered the last gem scale," said Tiblo.

"Excellent work," said the general. "Come to my office, I must speak with you."

"Alright," said Tiblo. "Captain Tigro out." He turned off his communicator. "Come on, scouts. The general needs us." He led the others down the hall and they all walked to the general's office.

CHAPTER 7

THE GENERAL'S NEWS

And so, the freedom fighters met up with the general in his office.

"What is your command, sir?" asked Tiblo.

"I have some good news and some bad news," said the general.

"Bad news first," said Tiblo.

"Alright," said the general, "now the thing was right when you collected those gem scales, they bring the Death Scale back together. Now our enemies will be strong and powerful again. So, if you continue your destiny, freedom fighters, you must defend us from everything that happens."

"This guy is a bear of bad news," said Skinamar. "Er, a bear-*er*."

"What about the good news?" asked Martino.

"I lied, there are no good news," said the general.

"Well, you shouldn't lie, it's bad," said Manda.

"Manda, he knows what he's talking about," said Tiblo.

"Whatever is it you want us to do, sir?" asked Regulto.

"Destroy whatever gets in the way," said the general.

"As you wish, general," said Tiblo. The freedom fighters left the office and walked back to the Great Red Shark in the hangar bay.

"So, what will our destiny be like?" asked Martino.

"Well, it depends," said Tiblo. "It will either be good or bad."

"We'll see for sure," said Skinamar.

Suddenly, an alarm rang out loud. Skinamar screamed and covered his ears. Asteroids were floating around the station. They bumped into it, making dents on top.

"I better check that out," said Tiblo, running by the lockers to rent a space suit.

"I'm coming with you," said Manda as she followed Tiblo.

"Me, too," said Shana. They all put on suits and floated out into space. They climbed up to the top of the hangar bay on jagged corners and ladder bars. They suddenly spotted a green substance staining part of the station. Manda gasped. "What is that stuff?!" she asked.

"Looks like it came from an alien of some kind," said Shana, "from deepest space."

Tiblo went to it and grabbed it with miniature laboratory tongs from his pack.

"Just as I suspected," he said, "a foreign planetary substance unidentified." He carried it back to the station. The girls followed him.

Back in the hangar bay, Skinamar said, "Should they be back by now?"

"I suppose so," said Martino.

"I see them," said Regulto as Tiblo, Shana, and Manda reappeared at the top of the giant doorway. They landed on the floor and took off their rented suits putting them back in the lockers. Tiblo carried the tongs with the green stuff and showed it to the others.

"What is that?" asked Martino.

"A rare alien substance," said Tiblo. "It came from a distance in space somewhere out there."

"Now, that's foreign and predictable," said Skinamar.

"I wonder where it came from," said Shana.

"We're about to find out," said Tiblo.

Suddenly, an old scientist cat called, Professor Fester Whiskey, arrived at the discovery made by the heroes.

"Well now, what have you got?" he asked Tiblo.

"A green substance of some kind," said Tiblo. He gave the tongs with the substance to the professor.

I thought he was colorblind, thought Martino. These animals really are that humanized.

"Follow me," said the professor. The freedom fighters followed him to a laboratory a few doors from the hangar. As they got there, the professor set a speck of the substance on a slide, which he set on the stage of a microscope. He looked through it and found tiny symbols of an unspoken language. He assumed it was a message.

"Of course!" he said. "This has some sort of meaning." Tiblo took the eye piece and looked inside.

"Just as I suspected!" he said. "An alien message saying that we will have a new enemy."

"Like what?" asked Martino. "Who would send such a message?"

"Who knows?" said Tiblo.

CHAPTER 8

A NEW ENEMY

Tiblo was right to worry. In outer space far away was a UFO occupied by aliens mixed with other genetics from a laboratory. The laboratory was owned by a scientist named, Dr. Brain Tenderborne. He was mixed with a giant brain that attached to his head. His two assistants, Grick and McGriggle, were mixed up, too. Grick was formed with a green skin with three eyes, long pointed ears and a patch of red hair. McGriggle was mixed as a fish-like monster with one slit eye, webbed hands and feet, a fin-line on his head and a fine-lined tail. They were once earthly humans until the mutation cause from different alien substances. Dr. Brain Tenderborne was later called, Brain Tentacles. He was mixed with three eyestalks pointing forward, a beard of octopus-like tentacles (where he got his new title), a thorax of a humanoid substance with a brown lab jacket, a right arm with a tongue plant[1] for a hand, and a left arm with a stainless steel crustacean claw. His abdomen was a cyborg of three odd legs: one was a multi-jointed droid leg, one was one of his own human legs, and another was a flat-footed robot leg.

1. Tongue plant-any various plants with a frog-like tongue for catching prey.

Brain Tentacles sat in a large chair as his assistants researched the laboratory's new mutant life forms.

"The galaxy is mine in my new alien form," said Brain Tentacles, starting his speech. He called to his assistants, "Grick! Check my new henchmen." Grick went to the bio-lab to see the alien developments.

"McGriggle!" Brain Tentacles called out. "Where is my destination for our missing phantom gem?"

"It's in a distance on a jungle planet that is unidentified," said McGriggle. "After your wife's death the gem must have fallen down where no one can find it."

Brain Tentacles grabbed his slit nose with his crustacean claw, squeezing the middle bar between the nostrils. McGriggle screamed in pain as Brain Tentacles squished it. McGriggle started giggling, and then he said, "It is probably a buried treasure right now." Brain Tentacles lowered his claw.

Grick arrived back in with his partner and boss. "All the aliens have been installed in new forms," he said.

"Excellent," said Brain Tentacles. "Before my wife died, she carried that gem and placed it in a canister and buried it. All we need is to locate its current position."

"Yes, boss," said McGriggle.

"First," said Brain Tentacles, "we have six heroes working for a peace-keeping team known as the Heaven Federation. They must know about our purpose. And when they follow our path, we'll be ready for them." Grick and McGriggle went back to the lab to check on the aliens working for their leader.

"Let's see, we've got . . ." McGriggle explained pointing and looking at the following mixed aliens. ". . . Cyglimpse . . ." Cyglimpse was a one-eyed alien with a goblin-like head and trunks for arms and legs. ". . . Rumble Bog . . ." Rumble Bog was a blue crocodile-like alien with one large middle eye, bent eyestalks on the sides of his head, and a plated shell with spider-like legs sticking out of his back. "Mr. Barfer . . ." Mr. Barfer was an orange, pot-bellied alien with a white suit, four legs with webbed feet, a large right eye, three small left eyes forming a triangle, a mouth of anemone-like tentacles, and a back-strapped tank with a sickening gas spread to make an enemy sick, causing him or her to vomit (that's why they call him "Mr. Barfer"). ". . . Vraught . . ." Vraught was an alien hybrid of an ant and a scorpion with pincer-hands, six walking legs, a scorpion's metasoma, and an ant's head. ". . . Qwreng . . ." Qwreng was a mud-bodied alien with alien plant leaves hanging from the sides of his head. ". . . Ugalf . . ." Ugalf was a bulldog-faced alien with rocked columns on his head forming a brain and tiny shrimp-like legs. ". . . Spongeface . . ." Spongeface was a fly-headed alien with a standard alien body. His name came from the fly's sponge-like mouth. ". . . Cephalo and Torsus . . ." Cephalo and Torsus were two different aliens forming one body. Cephalo was the head with a trunked mouth, horizontal-pupil eyes, a snail's shell for a helmet, and tentacles for staying on top of his partner, Torsus. Torsus was the whole body with his horizontal-pupil eyes on where nipples were supposed to be and his mouth at where a belly button should be. His feet had two toes each. ". . . Gumbar . . ." Gumbar was a fat red alien with a tuatara-like body and a grouper-like head with four yellow eyes, a head's fin-line, a pair of ear fins, and a large mouth with three tongues. ". . . and finally, Hizzly . . ." Hizzly was a snake-like alien with one slit eye, two forked tongues, two narrow arms and a pair of bat-like wings.

"Wow, what a great army we have!" said Grick in excitement.

"So," said Cyglimpse, "when do we start working for Brain Tentacles?"

"Immediately," said McGriggle. He and Grick went back to Brain Tentacles in his room.

"Before my wife's death," said Brain Tentacles, "she gave me this." He spread out a tentacle showing a microchip. "This chip is the key to the canister containing the galactic ghost gem. Whoever holds this shall reveal the 'Phantom of the Galaxy'."

"This is going to be exciting," said Grick.

"Shut up," said McGriggle.

CHAPTER 9

THE REAPPEARANCE OF A LOST CIVILIAN

Meanwhile, back in the Heavenly Federal station, the freedom fighters discovered a video chip that they found from the green substance. It contained complex video files. The heroes inserted the chip in a video projector in a laboratory by the meeting room. They turned it on and showed pictures of selectable videos. Many of them were about genetic transfers of alien DNA. The freedom fighters' purpose was to find out the one who sent the message. Manda pressed the right arrow button to find a scientist mentioned about the situation. They have heard of Brain Tentacles. As Manda kept searching, all she could see were pictures of DNA transfers.

"I can't find it," she said. "It appears to be nowhere on this chip."

"Well, keep looking," said Tiblo, "we'll get to it."

"I think the problem is that you're going too slow," said Skinamar to Manda. "Here, let me take the wheel, I'm a professional." Manda scooted away as Skinamar repeatedly pressed the right arrow button with speed, skimming through the menu.

"You're going to fast," said Shana. "No one can even tell what's here or there."

"Don't worry, I can tell," said Skinamar. He kept skimming until he accidentally skipped a video with the word "brain".

"Wait, go back!" shouted Martino and Tiblo simultaneously.

"That was it," said Martino alone.

"Alright, I'm going back," said Skinamar as he starting repeatedly pressing the left arrow button back to the previous menu videos. He kept doing it until the others shouted, "STOP! STOP! This is it."

They watched that video. It said, "Dr. Brain Tenderborne was a mad scientist who tested alien genetic transfers. He had the father brain stored in a tank until his body was mutated with acids of unknown organisms. His head was mixed with the brain. His body changed with parts of aliens and robots. His wife was killed with an alien's poison. Dr. Tenderborne's assistants Grick and McGriggle put her in a liquid container which was carried away to a distant planet. Mrs. Tenderborne was put in a liquid sleep to keep her alive."

"Crazy!" said Martino.

"It's like Jekyll and Hyde for Dr. Tenderborne," said Regulto.

The video continued," Mutant aliens are being created . . ." It showed all the mixed aliens being formed. "Dr. Brain Tenderborne is now called 'Brain Tentacles' because of growing a beard of squid-like tentacles.

"The aliens' purpose is to seek a galactic gem that contains the Phantom of the Galaxy hidden and sealed inside. It was held in a canister. Once it was claimed, the Heaven Federation hid it away." The video ended. Tiblo turned off the projector.

"Brain Tenderborne becomes Brain Tentacles?" said Shana.

"That's our guy," said Tiblo. "We'll wait for him anytime." Soon it was time to sleep. The freedom fighters went to the sleep chambers where they entered columns with sleeping gas, instantly putting them to sleep. Then they were knocked into hard beds. They all deeply dreamt.

Earthly hours passed. Tiblo could no longer sleep when he heard a splashing sound of slime coming from another room. Tiblo followed that sound and went into a hole under a metal floorboard. He found a trail of slime clear as syrup. There appeared a rather old wolf revived with alien substances such as tiny villi outside around his fur, an alien honeycomb on the right side of his face with a red pupil black eye, and a rough skinned right arm that is not really his.

"Captain Tiblo Tigro," said the wolf, "I bring you the ultimate news."

"What kind of news?" Tiblo asked.

"My new master, Brain Tentacles, sent me to see one of you freedom fighters," said the wolf. "I must give you this." He handed Tiblo a message plate on which he pressed a button to show the hologram of a key card.

"It's a hologram of a card," said Tiblo.

"This card is the key to what holds the galactic ghost gem," said the wolf.

"The Phantom of the Galaxy."

"I believe you have my daughter well-trained in battle."

"Your daughter? Manda??"

"Yes."

"You're Genghis Monka, aren't you."

"Yes."

"You've been dead for years."

"Take this to Brain Tentacles." Genghis Monka set out his false right arm and placed the hand on Tiblo's paw spread out. There came a green algae-like substance that formed a green bush on Tiblo's palm. It sealed itself within as a spot.

"A green splurge," said Tiblo.

"It is for a return message that must go to him," said Genghis. Tiblo started to leave.

"Thanks," he said.

"And, Tiblo," Genghis interrupted, "say 'hello' to my daughter for me."

"I will," said Tiblo.

Genghis turned into a sliding mound of sludge and disappeared through a vent going back into space to return to where he came from. Tiblo left the basement as he stared at the green spot in his palm. He inserted his paw into his trousers' hip pocket and rejoined his scouts in the bed chambers.

CHAPTER 10

THE REVIVAL PLAN

After that long sleep, the freedom fighters climbed aboard the Great Red Shark. Tiblo started to run the engine. The ship flew out of the hangar bay.

"Our destination is to find Brain Tentacles in space," he said to his scouts.

"This is going to be difficult," said Skinamar.

"It can be dangerous," said Manda.

"He's a monster," said Regulto.

"Calm down, everyone," said Martino.

Suddenly, the communication machine on a nearby desk beeped. Martino answered it. He pressed the button and out came Artidector's hologram.

"Guys!" Martino called out. "It's Artidector."

"Freedom fighters!" said Artidector. "I sense that your destination will be more difficult than you will expect. I have a plan that can help you farther. I shall revive some dead heroes that existed before. Meet me at the moon ahead." The hologram vanished.

"More heroes?" asked Martino.

"Why would we need that?" asked Shana.

"Just to make our quest easier, I guess," said Skinamar.

"Let's go see him," said Tiblo as he drove the ship to a white moon ahead. He landed the ship in a nearby crater. There was no atmosphere to breathe, so the freedom fighters put on space suits. They finally met up with Artidector outside the crater.

"Just in the right time," said Artidector.

"What news do you have for us, Artidector?" asked Tiblo.

"Climb on my back," said Artidector. "We must fly to Earth."

And so, Artidector flew the freedom fighters far away to planet Earth. The first stop was in the jungles of Africa. Artidector flew down there. All around were old world monkeys, snakes, parrots, insects, etc.

"Hey, monkeys!" Skinamar called out. "Did y'all miss me?"

Artidector dropped the freedom fighters down and said, "You must find Nala Boomer's grave, so I can revive her."

"Really?" asked Martino. "You want to bring a former heroine back to life?"

"Just find it," said Artidector.

"Come on," Tiblo said to the others. The freedom fighters walked a long way along a path in the jungle. It was until they found a pack of lions resting on rocks. One lion woke up and roared at the intruders and jumped in front of them. It roared again.

"I'll handle this," said Skinamar. He went to the lion and spoke to him. "We're looking for the grave of the lioness named, Nala Boomer."

"Really??" the lion spoke. "I am her father by the way. I'll show you her grave." The freedom fighters followed the lion across the savanna. A few trees were standing by. Suddenly, they found a mound of dirt with a stone painted in mud a picture of a lioness cub. Next to it was a blaster.

"Here it is," said the lion.

"This is definitely it!" said Skinamar. He picked up the blaster to see if it still worked. He aimed it at the ground and pulled the trigger. It blasted a smoking hole. "It still works."

"Artidector told us to take Nala to him so he can revive her," said Tiblo.

"Did he??" said the lion thinking. He dug into the grave until he found a white sack under the ground. It contained his daughter's dead body. "Here she is, my daughter in your hands."

Artidector suddenly flew overhead of the freedom fighters and landed on the ground.

"Over here, Artidector!" Martino called out. Artidector came to the heroes. Tiblo brought out his laser knife and cut the sack open to reveal the dead Nala Boomer.

"Ugh!" cried Shana grabbing her nose. "Why are we doing this?!"

"You will see why in a little time," said Artidector. He took Nala's body from the sack and used his magic powers to bring her back to life. "It will be time for her to continue her destiny while you continue yours, freedom fighters." Boomer's soul came to her body and Artidector healed the choked neck from the hangman's noose of the Serpentials' Spruce Noose. She could breathe once again. Artidector set her on the ground and she stood up on her hind paws.

"Nala Boomer is back!" shouted Skinamar.

"What happened?" asked Boomer speaking out.

"You have been brought back to life," said Artidector.

"Artidector??" Boomer asked as she turned back to him.

"Your destiny continues now in your second life," Artidector said.

"This is ridiculous," said Shana.

"We have more of our team than before," said Tiblo.

"I can't believe it's increasing," said Martino.

"It's not working out right," said Manda.

"Count me out," said Regulto.

"Come, freedom fighters," said Artidector. "Our next stop is Australia." He flew to that island at the east as the freedom fighters rode him.

"I thought Boomer's parents were dead a long time ago," said Martino.

"I guess it's just her mother who's dead," said Skinamar. "Hard to believe that her father's still alive, he must have survived that unknown disease."

"Well is he happy to see his daughter alive," said Martino, "and is she to *him* alive as well."

A moment passed as Artidector landed in Australia. The freedom fighters climbed off. Kangaroos were hopping everywhere.

"It's my homeland!" said Shana.

Artidector gave Nala Boomer her old outfit that she wore in the Heaven Federation's warfare back in her previous life. She was dressed up. Shana started hopping off.

"Shana!" Martino shouted. Tiblo heard him. He called out, "Shana, get back here!" Shana didn't hear him.

"Does anyone know me?" she tried asking the kangaroos.

"You seem familiar," said a male kangaroo nearby. "Who are you?"

"Shana Cargon," Shana answered. "A former member of this herd banished many years ago."

"Unbelievable," said another kangaroo.

"We better tell the chief," said a female kangaroo with them. The stranger kangaroos hopped away from Shana back to their herd.

Shana's wrist communicator beeped. She answered it. "Shana, get back to base." It was Tiblo's voice. Shana called the message back, "I'm on my way." She hopped back to the crew.

"Our purpose here is to find a dead man called, Steve Irwin," said Artidector, "a famous game hunter from a century ago, who was stabbed by a ray."

"Awkward," said Martino. Shana arrived back with the crew.

"There are plenty of friends of mine ahead," she said. "They might know what to tell us. Come on!" She led everybody to the savanna ahead.

"Is this really your homeland?" Manda asked Shana.

"It was," Shana answered.

"Who knows whether this is a little family reunion?" said Skinamar.

"It could be something cruel and dangerous," said Regulto.

As they all arrived in the plain with all the kangaroos, the head chief stood before them and started speaking, "Is it really my daughter, Shana?"

"Dad??" Shana said. She hopped to him. The chief hugged her. "You're the current chief?" Shana asked him.

"The previous one passed away a year ago," said her father, the current chief.

"So much for banishment for me as a joey," said Shana.

"I've held this while you were gone." The chief held a hand-built slingshot in his paw.

"My old slingshot! Don't worry, Dad, I have better weapons in my crew."

"Who's the large white bird?"

"That's Artidector. He's the god who took care of me and my friends."

The rest of the team walked forward to the herd.

"I'm Tiblo Tigro," said Tiblo introducing himself, "captain of the Heaven Federation."

"My name's Martino Izodorro," said Martino.

"I'm Skinamarinky-Dinky-Dink Skinamarinky-Doo," said Skinamar.

"Hey, that's an old song," said one of the kangaroos.

"Yes, and now I own that name," said Skinamar.

"I'm Regulto Beauxon," said Regulto. "I have an alter ego named, Rufus, who is a beast, so beware."

"I'm Manda Monka," said Manda.

"Welcome to our herd," said the chief. "What is your purpose here?"

"Artidector said something about a famous hunter who died a long time ago," said Tiblo.

"I think his name was Steve . . ." said Martino trying to remember, ". . . Irwin."

"I've heard amazing stories about him long ago," said the chief. "I can lead you to his grave." He started hopping to a certain path as the freedom fighters followed him. Artidector flew overhead.

They all ended up in an old side town blasted with smoke.

"It's a ghost town," said Martino. "And it looks completely deserted."

"Of course it's deserted," said Skinamar. "Every human on Earth had to flee from upcoming dangers that arrived."

"That must have been the Sharp Empire," said Manda.

"My point exactly," said Martino. "No wonder my aunt and uncle died when I went back home for something."

"I created my own last name, 'Beauxon', when my parents died," said Regulto. "My father's last name was Raxon, from England, and my mother's last name was Beaujour, from France."

"This is the graveyard of the Irwin family," said the chief.

"We gotta find the right person," said Martino.

"He must be around here somewhere," said Tiblo as his nose twitched. He sniffed around the graves. Skinamar searched grave by grave for the right Irwin person. He found the grave that said "Steve Irwin: Famous Television Crocodile Hunter (1962-2006)".

"I found it!" Skinamar called out.

"Finally!" said Martino and Regulto.

"Good work, Skinamar," said Manda.

"Let's dig it up," said Tiblo.

"Not again," said Shana.

The freedom fighters grabbed some nearby shovels and started digging into the grave. As they did, Artidector flew above and landed on the graveyard's ground. This went on and on until one shovel hit something solid. The heroes uncovered it. It was Steve Irwin's coffin.

"Let's bring it out," said Tiblo. The freedom fighters lifted the coffin out of the grave.

"I can't believe we're doing this," said Regulto.

"This thing is heavy!" said Martino with his teeth pushing.

They set the coffin on the upper ground. They opened it with the appearance of Irwin's dead body. Artidector studied him. He sealed and healed the stabbed heart and brought his soul back to his body.

"This is like Frankenstein's piracy," said Shana.

"Steve Irwin," said Artidector, "arise." Steve Irwin awoke for his new second life. He opened his eyes.

"WHOA!" he shouted. "Crikey. What are you?!"

"I am the condor god of fear conquerable and courage to be sought," said Artidector. "The name is Artidector. And I have brought you some new friends."

Steve Irwin looked behind him. "I see two humans, and the others are animals standing on their hind paws and wearing clothing from some industrial company," he said.

"We are the freedom fighters of the Heaven Federation up in space," said Tiblo introducing the crew. "I'm Captain Tiblo Tigro."

"I'm Martino Izodorro," said Martino.

"I'm Skinamarinky-Dinky-Dink Skinamarinky-Doo," said Skinamar.

"I'm Regulto Beauxon," said Regulto.

"I'm Shana Cargon," said Shana.

"And I'm Manda Monka," said Manda.

"And this is my new life?" Irwin asked.

"Come with us and we shall fulfill your destiny," said Artidector. He used his talon hands to form a clear ball and put it around Irwin.

"Oy!" said Irwin. "I'm inside a giant bubble!"

"We are going to outer space," said Artidector. "You will have that bubble for breathing oxygen."

The freedom fighters put on their space suits as Artidector put another clear ball around Nala Boomer. They rode on Artidector's back. Artidector held Boomer and Irwin within his arms as he flew back to the moon. Artidector gave them spacesuits that he made himself. The freedom fighters climbed off his back and boarded the Great Red Shark again.

"What will you do with Boomer and Irwin?" Martino asked Artidector.

"I must hold onto them and train them," Artidector answered.

"Good luck, old comer and newcomer," said Tiblo as he started the Great Red Shark engines. The six freedom fighters flew away.

CHAPTER 11

ARTIDECTOR'S TRAINING

Beginning to train the revived heroes, Artidector set an obstacle course around a large crater. Boomer and Irwin interacted.

"I'm Steve Irwin," said Irwin. "Who are you? You look like a lioness."

"I'm Nala Boomer," said Boomer. "I was once a freedom fighter of the Heaven Federation until I was held up for execution by our enemy, the Sharp Empire."

"Sharp Empire?" said Irwin. "Hm . . ." He put his hand on his helmet's glass. "I've never been in space before, but whatever that empire is, it's gonna be a relief to have a second life."

"You'll get used to it someday," said Boomer.

"I just can't believe we're on the moon," said Irwin. Artidector finished setting up the course for running.

"Now let us move on," he said. "The first event is running and your tricks. Go!"

"Tricks?" said Irwin.

"Come on, let's move!" said Boomer as they started running slowly.

"This is slow motion," said Irwin.

"The moon's gravity is weaker than Earth's," said Boomer.

"Oh, I get it!" said Irwin. "I get to go up higher." They ran into a giant hurdle and started flipping over it about 8 feet high. Just then, Artidector appeared in front of them.

"Excellent work," he said. "You have passed the first test. The next test is firing at the enemy." He set out dinosaur and bird-shaped dummies and gave Boomer and Irwin blasters.

"I've never used guns like these," said Irwin. He looked at the dummies ahead. "Birds, giant lizards, and crocodiles? Oh, crikey."

"Aim directly at your enemies to pass this test," said Artidector.

Boomer and Irwin started shooting the dummies as Artidector switched them with new ones shaped like robots, monsters and others.

CHAPTER 12

THE HENCHMONSTER BASE

And so, the freedom fighters flew back to space. Tiblo remembered to find the Forbidden UFO out somewhere in the distance. As the freedom fighters searched around they entered the Death Scale's system and landed on a purple planet of nuclear gases.

"Where are we?" asked Tiblo.

The Invisi-Bot came up and said, "We are on the nuclear planet, Nucleorg, the second planet distant from the Death Scale."

"Great," said Tiblo.

"Does this have anything to do with our mission?" asked Martino as he went up to Tiblo in the cockpit.

"Not exactly," Tiblo said. "But we're about to look." He got out of the pilot's seat and called out for the others. "Scouts! We have a planet under our feet." The other freedom fighters climbed out of their seats and followed Tiblo off the ship and onto the surface.

"We'll need gas masks," said Tiblo. Everybody dug in their backpacks for gas masks.

"Good idea," said Martino.

"That's what I need to hear about," said Skinamar. The freedom fighters found their masks and put them on.

"Now what do we do here?" asked Shana.

"We've got exploring to do," said Tiblo. They all started walking.

"This place is too hazy," said Manda looking around at yellow and green gases.

"I wish Rufus was here," said Regulto.

"Just follow the empty plains," said a growling voice in front of him. It was Rufus the beast.

"Yes," said Regulto.

A few minutes passed. The freedom fighters found a building about twice the size of the blue whale.

"What is this place?" asked Martino.

Tiblo called the Invisi-Bot through his communicator. "Invisi-Bot, use the monitor to identify this building."

"This building is the base of Emperor Sharp's henchmonsters," said the Invisi-Bot. "If you look inside you will see every monster you have ever fought before."

"Captain Tigro sailing off," Tiblo turned off his communicator. "Let's head inside."

"It's going to be dangerous," said Manda.

"Just follow me," said Tiblo. "We'll be sure to find something." The freedom fighters walked into the entrance door ahead of them.

"This is not going to be a pretty picture, I can tell," said Skinamar.

"Good thing I remembered about my medicine," said Regulto. The freedom fighters entered the doorway. They walked through the inside hallways in search of clues.

Deeper inside, the henchmonsters, Lava Lobster, Monstrous Slug, Junky the Bulldog, Long-Tailed Skeleton, Clown Coach, Scorpionyx, and all the others from before were planning a strategy.

"Those freedom fighters shall no longer stand a chance, mateys," said Lava Lobster.

"I'll scare them away with slime and mucus," said Monstrous Slug.

"Who's ready to clown around now?" said Clown Coach.

"Destroy those freedom fighters!" said Scorpionyx.

"Electrocute them!" said Sparxcalibur.

"I can't taste as good this time!" said the Jamba Juice Glob.

"This time, we clobber them!" said the fighting lizards.

"I see them!" said Three Heads, using a nearby alert computer. "They're coming this way into our ballroom."

The freedom fighters finally entered the room. They all stood before the monsters as they all prepared themselves for combat. The freedom fighters took out their weapons.

"It's rampage time! Arrrgghhh!" roared Lava Lobster as he plunged his pincers into the floor creating fiery geysers. Tiblo flipped back and repeatedly shot his twin blasters. Manda twisted in sidesteps as she waved her new light saber. Monstrous Slug splattered his slime. The

Jamba Juice Glob oozed around. Skinamar tried tasting him but he no longer tasted good.

"Lech!" Skinamar held his mouth open with his tongue hanging. "So much for a free beverage."

"Skinamar, stop goofing around, we gotta keep fighting!" said Martino.

"That's what I'm trying to do around here!" said Skinamar.

Sparxcalibur used his lightning to strike the power to overrun it inside the room. Flashes of light blinked everywhere. Shana used her hyper-powered boomerang to strike his arm, slicing it off.

"Argh!" Sparxcalibur shouted.

"Let's try running a cool set," said Shana. She brought a pair of jumper cables. She attached one end on a metal rod. "Hey, Manda!" she called. "Grab another rod like this and give it to the monsters, then grab that cable and pinch it on."

"Alright!" Manda responded. She grabbed the other end of the cable and attached it on another nearby metal rod. She lured the monsters to it. Lava Lobster, Monstrous Slug, and Three Heads, grabbed it together. Shana threw the other rod at Sparxcalibur who was reattaching his arm. The rod plunged into his chest absorbing all the powerful lightning from his body. It conducted many waves of it and it flowed through the cable to the rod with the other monsters. They were all electrocuted. Seconds later, Sparxcalibur exploded; all that was left was his body's framework. Lava Lobster, Monstrous Slug, and Three Heads were knocked back in black smoke.

Next came Grop oozing the floor. Tiblo stepped into his slime. Grop lifted his body up and frowned. He planted vines around the freedom fighters. Long-Tailed Skeleton appeared along with Plag and Junky the Bulldog. Plant bulbs grew on the vines. Tiblo grabbed one and threw it toward Grop's head. Grop lowered his body into the ground like a puddle of ooze. Long-Tailed Skeleton caught the bulb and dropped it. Plag opened his mouth and spread out green plague methane. The freedom fighters ducked for cover from the plague. Tiblo put on his gas mask. He found a nearby giant glass window. He waved his arms for the henchmonsters to spot him. Long-Tailed Skeleton took off his right arm and threw it at Tiblo like a bola. Junky the Bulldog barked. Tiblo caught Long-Tailed Skeleton's arm.

"Here, boy!" he called Junky while waving the arm. Junky barked and started running to him. Tiblo threw the arm at the glass window. Junky ran into it and broke the glass.

"Give me back my arm!" called Long-Tailed Skeleton.

Tiblo went back for his scouts. "We have a way out," he said. The others put on their gas masks. They all moved through the plague by the giant window.

"Smart move, Tiblo," said Martino.

"I always wanted a broken window for an escape way," said Skinamar.

Junky went back with Long-Tailed Skeleton's arm back in the ballroom. The freedom fighters ended up what appeared to be a dark, empty sport gym.

"Too dark to see a thing or two," said Regulto. The freedom fighters took off their gas masks. Lights were suddenly turned on. More henchmonsters arrived. There appeared Brocker, Ice Brain, Mega Hawk, and Stargoyle. Brocker slammed the floor with his clawed fists, creating a crack running toward the heroes. They jumped away from it. Mega Hawk squawked and formed an egg-shaped nuclear grenade with his talons. He flew overhead.

"This is bad," said Martino.

"Double bad," said Skinamar.

"Prepare to become ice statues, freedom fighters!" said Ice Brain. He pointed his ice blaster at the freedom fighters.

"Whirlwind power!" shouted Stargoyle above, blowing a tornado. The freedom fighters fled everywhere. Regulto was caught in the tornado. He struggled to fight it. He slowly reached into a side pocket for his medicine. He drank it and turned into Rufus the beast. As he transformed, he roared and fell to the floor. He spun himself around to reverse the tornado, bringing Stargoyle to the ground.

"Yoooouuuuu fooooolll!" said Stargoyle as he was brought down. As he touched the ground, he started a wrestling match with Rufus. He smacked his spiked tail club on the floor to cause an earthquake. Rufus grappled with him and they pushed each other. The other heroes trembled from the earthquake.

"You're finished," said Rufus. He flipped over Stargoyle and grabbed his tail. He swung him around and threw him at a wall about 15 feet away. Stargoyle crashed and caused a crack in it. The wall felt weak.

"You'll regret this," said Stargoyle. He turned around and shot a couple of lightning curve sparks from the corners of his mouth. Rufus used a solid fist to break a crack in the wall. The lightning went into it and flowed along the cracking lines. It went up toward Mega Hawk and straight toward Brocker. Brocker roared and raised his arms then got electrocuted. Mega Hawk flew down and activated his grenade. He dropped it. Rufus grabbed it and threw it back at Mega Hawk. The grenade exploded. Mega Hawk was covered in purple nuclear gas. Ice Brain suddenly froze all the other freedom fighters.

"You're all in my hands now!" he said.

Rufus went toward them all. "We'll see about that!" he said. He picked up a nearby metal box and threw it at Ice Brain's tank holding his brain. It broke open and spilled the water out.

"You fiendish monster!" he said. He grew tentacles from his brain stem and started to rise up among Rufus. Ice Brain whipped several of his tentacles trying to fight him. Rufus grabbed a bundle of tentacles and started to swing Ice Brain around. He threw him at the same wall he threw Stargoyle at. There formed a hole. It nearly looked big enough. Rufus warmed up and made a hot breath to free the others from the ice. It melted.

"Whoa!" said Martino waking up. "What happened?"

"You were frozen," said Rufus.

"That Ice Brain must have used a freezing prank on us with his blaster," said Tiblo as he shook his fur dry.

Brocker showed up. His red eyes flashed showing his anger. He grabbed a loose pipe from nearby and used it like a Bo staff against the freedom fighters. Rufus wrestled against him.

"Go to the hole in the wall!" Rufus told the freedom fighters. They all ran to the broken wall. Rufus continued wrestling. He turned Brocker around and pulled hard on the pipe. Brocker was still stronger. Rufus fell backward and rejoined the heroes as they tried to escape. Rufus made the hole bigger. The freedom fighters ran back to the Great Red Shark as Regulto's medicine wore off and Rufus turned back to his human ego.

"I was lucky to get away from those monsters," said Martino.

"We could have gotten out of it ourselves," said Skinamar.

"Way to go, Rufus," said Regulto.

"Way to play Jekyll and Hyde," said Shana.

"Back on board," said Tiblo. The freedom fighters climbed aboard the Great Red Shark.

"Welcome back," said the Invisi-Bot. "How was everything?"

"A disaster," said Tiblo. "Does the Shark have enough fuel?"

"Dramatically yes," said the Invisi-Bot. "Wherever you're going there's always plenty I assure."

Tiblo entered the pilot's cockpit and started the ship and left the planet. The freedom fighters continued their search for the Forbidden UFO.

CHAPTER 13

THE RISE OF THE FATHER BRAIN

Meanwhile, the Serpential forces searched in another area of space for the freedom fighters.

"They appear to be far off," said Captain Kerbano Kassow.

"We must scan the entire galaxy," said Darth Waternoose. He used his time vision to see where the freedom fighters were and what they were up to.

"Lord Waternoose," said Admiral Marwick MacFnurd. "An alien ship is somewhere bringing the Heaven Federation messages of strange elements."

"They are meeting aliens of combined genetics," said Waternoose. "They must not be allowed to go any farther."

"My lord," said an upcoming Serpential officer. "The emperor brings you a message." Waternoose followed the officer to a communication room inside that scale destroyer, a large ship with powerful laser beam cannons. As Waternoose entered the communication room, the emperor's hologram appeared.

"What is thy bidding, master?" Waternoose asked.

"We have a former enemy brought back to life by Artidector's powers," said the emperor.

"It is Nala Boomer I seek," said Waternoose. "She is revived to continue her quest against us."

"You know the truth of a previous life," said the emperor. "You should learn what's within a new life. Search your feelings, Lord Waternoose."

"She will join us or die, as you command."

"As I agreed, she can be a use to us."

"The Death Scale is completely together again."

"Excellent. Now I shall rule again." The emperor's hologram vanished. Waternoose left the room to rejoin the officers' search for the freedom fighters.

And so, the freedom fighters finally witnessed an alien UFO on the monitor.

"This has to be him," said Tiblo.

"Brain Tentacles?" asked Martino and Skinamar.

"Yep," said Tiblo. "He's right in our sight." The UFO appeared ahead of the Great Red Shark.

"That *is* the UFO," said Manda. "I sense somebody familiar is there somewhere."

"Either that's your imagination, Manda," said Martino, "or the Force is playing tricks on you."

"I must volunteer to discover that ship," said Manda.

"Alright," said Tiblo. "You fly over there and see what those aliens want with us."

"I have your orders," said Manda leaving down to the hangar bay for her ship.

"Be careful out there!" said Skinamar. "We don't want a slime popsicle for a comrade."

Manda flew out of the Great Red Shark's hangar in the Marine Wolf. She headed for the Forbidden UFO.

"She better be safe on her way back," said the Invisi-Bot.

As Manda flew into the UFO's docking bay, there were patches of foreign scum and contaminants, oozing on the walls. There were skeletons of intruders from other planets lying under the walls where the scum ate their flesh and internal organs. Manda jumped out of her ship and lit her light saber and roasted the scum blobs off the walls. Meanwhile, the mutant mixed aliens realized they had an intruder on their ship. Rumble Bog, Qwreng, Vraught, and Ugalf walked down to see the trouble. Manda destroyed all of the dreaded scum blobs as they smoked and fell off the walls.

"Hey!" said Rumble Bog. "A foreign female creature from another planet."

"Surprise surprise," said Vraught. Manda turned to the aliens and waved her light saber.

"Whoa!" said the aliens.

"We won't hurt you," said Rumble Bog.

"We'll just take you to our master," said Qwreng.

As they walked up the slope with Manda, Brain Tentacles appeared walking around tanks containing life forms about to be terminated. He faced a tank with a green amphibian shivering in fear. Brain Tentacles smoked a pipe and blew out smoke from his siphons.

"This creature is about to be terminated at the point of his intrusion," he said. He grabbed the specimen out of its tank. Another foreign alien spoke out behind him, "You are not of a true keeper of biological forms." Brain Tentacles grabbed his neck with his steel crustacean claw choking him.

"You somewhat defy me, stranger," said Brain Tentacles. "Grick, McGriggle."

"Yes, sir," said Grick and McGriggle responding.

"Take these two specimens into the chamber of reaction," Brain Tentacles commanded. Grick and McGriggle took the green amphibian and the foreign standing alien away.

"Master!" said the other mixed aliens. "We have an intruder here with us." They brought Manda forward.

"You are somehow new here," said Brain Tentacles as he approached her. "You are neither captured nor expected. What is your purpose here?"

"My captain sent me here to negotiate with you for your messages," Manda explained.

"What is that??" Brain Tentacles asked.

"My leader," Manda said, "Tiblo Tigro sent me here about your messages."

Brain Tentacles laughed. Then so did most of the aliens.

"Take me to your captain," Brain Tentacles commanded Manda. Manda led him down to the hangar bay and she entered her ship while Brain Tentacles had a flying saucer where he fitted his body in a vase-like pod and a glass closed over his head. He followed Manda back to the Great Red Shark. They entered its hangar bay. They climbed out of their ships.

"I'll take it from here," said Brain Tentacles. He walked up the railway alone as he left Manda standing next to her ship. Manda secretly followed Brain Tentacles where he went. Up in the top deck, he confronted Tiblo.

"You have my message, Captain Tigro?" he asked.

"Yes," said Tiblo. "This." He showed his paw with the green spot. Manda arrived at the scene where she saw it from the back. Brain Tentacles set his tongue plant hand's tongue on the spot and removed it. It shrank and disappeared.

"It is cured," said Brain Tentacles.

Tiblo noticed Manda peeking at the moment. He took out the message plate from his trousers' hip pocket and tossed it all the way to her. Brain Tentacles witnessed it. Manda caught the plate and hid from Brain Tentacles' sight.

"I believe Manda will be needing that for something," said Tiblo.

"Excellent," said Brain Tentacles. "I'll be leaving." He walked away and turned into slime oozing away down to the hangar bay for his pod. Manda quickly ran down there for her ship. They were both gone back to the Forbidden UFO. It was up to Manda to figure out the next clue for the mission.

CHAPTER 14

FATHER AND DAUGHTER REUNION

Strange feelings continued to rise in Manda's mind as she was held prisoner in the Forbidden UFO. Research appeared on nearby computers. There was a text about a disease called UBDD (Unidentified Body-Dwelling Disease). Manda assumed it was the disease that killed Nala Boomer's mother before Nala was hired in the Heaven Federation.

And so, the mixed aliens worked around the ship. They kept the place cleaned up and together as one large vehicle. Power generators warmed up and the ship was headed for wherever the galactic ghost gem was hidden.

"Our mission awaits another day of light," Brain Tentacles explained. "Keep up the generators, boys!"

Manda snuck from the top balcony to peer down at the aliens working.

"Where is Mr. Monka?!" Brain Tentacles asked in rage. Genghis Monka appeared around an upper room. Manda tried running downstairs to hide. Genghis showed up and headed down there, too. As Manda tried to hide, Genghis looked around and he and Manda saw each other face to face. Manda knew there was somebody familiar on the Forbidden UFO. And so, it was true. Genghis remembered his daughter's face correctly. He turned back to Brain Tentacles' call. Manda hid from the other aliens. Suddenly they found her in an expected matter of intrusion. They grabbed her and dragged her on a solid table. They lifted up her tunic to show her back of blue fur. Brain Tentacles walked to Genghis and asked, "Do you know this creature?"

"Yes, I know her," said Genghis.

"And what is her relationship with you?" asked Brain Tentacles.

"She's my daughter," said Genghis.

"Is that so?" Brain Tentacles lifted up a bar-like object that looked like a laser tube as long as a flashlight. "Here, use this on her." He gave it to Genghis.

"A light whip?" Genghis said. "No."

"Punish her with it!" Brain Tentacles growled.

"If you insist, Master." Genghis grabbed the light whip and turned it on by a button on it. It was lit with tiny sparks of laser light. He waved it backward as it showed a curving bar of light. He waved the light on his daughter's back creating a sparkling wound. He did it again in different areas about six more times. The aliens started laughing. Brain Tentacles frowned and growled with his mouth closed until it made a popping sound like a bubble. Genghis stopped whipping his daughter. Manda was bleeding in multiple areas. She ran up the stairway to find a bandage kit. Genghis dropped the light whip and followed her up there. Manda spread a sheet of absorbent cotton and rested on a bed with it under her to press on it and have it catch the blood. She took off her tunic and hung it on a nearby hook on the wall. Genghis showed up to see his daughter.

"Listen to me," he said.

"No," said Manda. "You're one of them right now!"

"You must trust me!" said Genghis. Manda rose off the bed and ran out of the hospital room. Genghis followed her. They ended up in the bio-form laboratory downstairs. "I wish to know your purpose here," Genghis said.

"I'm looking for this," Manda took out the message plate she got from Tiblo. She turned it on and it showed the hologram of the key chip.

"A microchip," said Genghis.

Suddenly, a nearby fish-like alien with arms and legs climbed out of his tank and looked at the hologram.

"The card chip to the galactic ghost gem?" he said.

"What do you know of this?" Manda asked him.

The fish-like alien explained, "That chip unlocks the canister hidden on a distant planet, which contains the gem. Sealed inside lies the Phantom of the Galaxy. Whatever you do, don't break the gem, otherwise the phantom will be free to haunt the galaxy and even the entire universe. He could threaten every living thing with many purposes. So make sure you keep the gem safe." He swam back in his tank.

"You'll have to wait," said Genghis to Manda. "To obtain that chip, you must challenge Brain Tentacles into stealing it. He holds the chip for the canister."

"I'll remember," said Manda.

"By the way," said Genghis quickly, "before your sister was murdered, I hid this emblem from the emperor."

"What is it?" asked Manda.

"It is the medal of our home planet which kept it safe from danger, until the emperor removed it. Take it. It will make you braver than before." Genghis gave it to Manda who obtained the medal that instant.

"Thank you," she said.

Meanwhile, the remaining five freedom fighters flew the Great Red Shark in search of the canister containing the gem, racing Brain Tentacles.

"That Brain Tentacles guy was really disgusting," said Shana.

"Relax," said Martino. "We must find that thing they're after, no matter what."

"This will be a blast without Manda," said Tiblo.

"Weird aliens, Manda's missing, a ghost inside a gem," said Skinamar. "We're doomed!"

"Don't be ludicrous, Skinamar," said Martino. "How long is she gonna be gone with those things?"

"Who knows?" said Regulto. "I don't believe anything bad will happen to her."

"She'll be alright," said Tiblo. "It will only be a matter of time when those aliens get there before us."

CHAPTER 15

A CHALLENGE FOR THE MICROCHIP

And so, as the Forbidden UFO continued its voyage, Brain Tentacles played an alien-built pipe organ with his beard of tentacles. Time passed as the aliens awoke from space sleep. It was time that Manda awoke, too. Down in the ship's deck, the aliens played gambling games with chips and cards. Some had jacks and marbles. Manda knew she had to challenge Brain Tentacles in one of those games. She went down the stairway along with her father.

"These games are very complicated to play, so you'll need the rules the aliens give you," said Genghis.

"I'll try to be patient," said Manda. She looked to the aliens down there and called out, "I challenge Brain Tentacles!"

The aliens turned to Manda up at the balcony saying, "Huh?!" one by one. Brain Tentacles marched into the room.

"I accept," he said. He walked toward the table where Manda and Genghis sat by.

"I shall join in," said Genghis. Brain Tentacles sat down in a chair across from Manda.

"This game is called 'Finder'," Brain Tentacles introduced the game to Manda. "We each start by dividing the deck into the number of parts equal to the number of players here. You call out for how many of the same picture on the cards and we show out our hands holding ten cards each. Then the game goes on counterclockwise to each player's turn." The three players grabbed ten cards from each of their decks.

"Allow me to start," said Brain Tentacles. "Four cogs." Manda showed her cards. She had four cards with cogs like Brain Tentacles said.

"The cards are mine," said Brain Tentacles as he collected those cards from Manda. "Since I got what I asked for, I go again. Five bats."

Manda looked at her hand of cards as she picked up four more cards. She had only one bat as Genghis had two. They showed their cards to Brain Tentacles.

"Now it's your turn, young Miss Monka," said Brain Tentacles.

"By the way, I came for this," Manda took out the message plate with the hologram of the card chip. Then she turned it on.

"Ah," said Brain Tentacles. He suddenly coughed and hacked and barfed out the microchip from his throat holding it between two of his three tongues. The chip was covered in slime from his mouth.

"She must not be allowed to have it," said Rumble Bog.

"She can't steal our property from us," said Cephalo hopping off of Torsus.

"Yeah," said Torsus. "She'll get away with it to reveal the Galactic Ghost."

Brain Tentacles swallowed the card chip, storing it in a pouch in his throat.

"Your turn!" he said to Manda again. So they continued the game.

"Five sponges," Manda said. Brain Tentacles had only three sponge cards and Genghis had the same number. Next it was Genghis' turn.

"Six leaves," he said. The others showed their cards, but no luck.

"Seven blobs," said Brain Tentacles. Neither one of the Monkas had those cards.

"This game is difficult," said Manda. "Five bats." Brain Tentacles had the five bat cards. He passed them to Manda.

"I resign," said Genghis.

"What?" Brain Tentacles asked.

"I resign," Genghis explained. "I must exit this game. My daughter can take the tie between both of you."

"Very well," said Brain Tentacles. "The game is mine, Monkas. By the way, Miss Monka, feel free to fly through

space with your friends while your father is still my slave."
He started laughing with all the other aliens.

"Well put, master," said Rumble Bog.

"Her lesson is learned," said Spongeface.

"Her access is denied," said Brain Tentacles.

"Why did you do that?" Manda asked her father.

"I wanted to warn you that he is a tricky beast," said
Genghis.

"No wonder," said Manda.

"I have a better plan," said Genghis. "Follow me."
Manda followed him back to the balcony.

Meanwhile, back to where the other freedom fighters
headed. They seemed far back behind the Forbidden
UFO.

"When are we ever gonna get Manda back?" asked
Regulto.

"As soon as she is done with those aliens," said Tiblo.

"We've gone so far and we'll never get through this,"
said Martino.

"Relax," Tiblo said. "We'll get there when we can."

Back on Earth's moon, Artidector was nearly finished
with training Nala Boomer and Steve Irwin.

"There is one thing you must achieve," Artidector said
to Boomer. "You shall take revenge on the Serpentials."

Nala entered an unknown cave under a shelf of the
moon's rocks. Her imagination turned on. Suddenly, an
illusion of Darth Waternoose appeared in the darkness.
Nala carried out her blaster. The illusion of Waternoose lit

his light saber. The fight began. Nala shot her blaster at the illusion repeatedly as the illusion blocked the shots with his light saber. He lunged at Nala as she dodged it, sidling to a wall. She shot the illusion's face and it malfunctioned and fell to the ground. The face exploded and inside was the face of a foreign human. Nala was astonished.

"So I have my revenge," she said as she walked out of the cave.

"Yes indeed," said Artidector.

Soon it was time for Steve Irwin's revenge. There came an illusion of a bull ray (the kind that killed him).

"Whoa, crikey!" Steve shouted.

"Use this against the illusion," said Artidector as he gave him a cylinder bar with a button activating sparks of light.

"What is it?" Steve asked.

"A light whip," said Artidector. "It is rumored as a laser-powered whip weapon."

As Steve activated the light whip, a green spark of light appeared. He waved it at the bull ray illusion with a flash of green light. The ray swiveled and vanished.

"So much for underwater studies in my previous life," Steve said.

"That is why revenge lies within you," said Artidector.

CHAPTER 16

OperATION TENTACLES

In the Forbidden UFO, Genghis had run a daring plan for his daughter.

"Now you must get that microchip yourself," he said.

"But how?" Manda asked. "Brain Tentacles has it swallowed."

"It does not stay in there for long," Genghis explained. "As he sleeps, he holds it in his tentacles. Be careful, as you try to grab it."

"It will be worth a try," said Manda. She had a pair of small tongs in her pack for grabbing the chip from Brain Tentacles' clutches. She went to the bottom of the chamber where Brain Tentacles lay asleep, reclining on a metal board used for dissection.

"Good luck," said Genghis.

Manda snuck inside the chamber, approaching Brain Tentacles. She searched for the microchip and found it within a curled tentacle pressing against Brain Tentacles' throat. Manda slowly and carefully reached the tongs at the tentacle moving other tentacles out of the way. As she touched the one with the chip, Brain Tentacles lifted his steel-clawed arm up and tapped on the side of the board he rested on. Manda quickly hid under the board as Brain Tentacles opened his eyes, about to awake. He closed his eyes and went back to sleep. Manda dug the tongs within the tentacles again. She finally touched the microchip, grasping it between the tongs. She carefully pulled the chip out of the tentacle. She placed it in her hip pocket and pulled out the message plate with the microchip's hologram. She placed it in the tongs' grip and placed it in the tentacle that held the microchip. Then she quietly snuck out of the chamber and rejoined her father.

"Mission accomplished," Manda said as she showed her father the microchip.

"Excellent," Genghis said. "Now you must escape."

"Escape is what I planned," said Manda. "But aren't you coming with me?"

"I must stay on this ship for if Brain Tentacles approaches the destined planet," said Genghis, "the aliens and I can guard the entrance to the gem's hidden zone until you and your friends arrive there."

"I hope we meet again," said Manda. She walked down to the UFO's hangar bay for her ship, sneaking past the sleeping aliens. She made it down there. She got into her ship. "Marine Wolf ready for takeoff?" she asked as she activated it.

"Acknowledged," said the computer. And so, Manda blasted off and made it out of the hangar.

CHAPTER 17

ESCAPE FROM THE UFO

So it was planned, Manda flew back for the other freedom fighters when suddenly, a series of asteroids blocked the path.

"I hope I'm not too late," she said. "I must tell the others the truth." There were too many asteroids around. Manda flew up to see something more clearly among them. It took quite a long time.

Meanwhile, back in the Forbidden UFO, Brain Tentacles and his alien minions awoke from their sleep. Brain Tentacles uncurled his tentacle that held the message plate and witnessed it as it was instead of holding the microchip.

"That meddlesome wolf double-crossed me for the last time," he said. "Send reinforcements!" he commanded his minions. "Find that she-wolf!"

The aliens saluted and obeyed his orders. They sent out robots and fired laser cannons at the asteroids to search for Manda. She suddenly found the Great Red Shark a few dozen yards away. She flew down there. Inside the Shark, the others witnessed the Marine Wolf diving into the horde of asteroids.

"I see Manda coming near us," said Tiblo. "She's still in danger." He drove the ship down to get Manda's attention. The aliens' laser cannons fired and missed the Marine Wolf. They shot down the asteroids in the way. Robots were crashing. Manda snuck under the asteroids and boosted straight under the Great Red Shark.

"No sign of that girl," said Mr. Barfer to Brain Tentacles. "She must've gone too far in deep space."

"Do not interfere," said Brain Tentacles. "We now have all the freedom fighters together as one team."

"Hallelujah," said McGriggle.

"There's a surprise," said Grick. "We're onto them for the gem."

"Looks like we'll have to use our brains," said Rumble Bog.

"I am the brain," said Brain Tentacles.

And so, both the Forbidden UFO and the Great Red Shark continued the voyage to the faraway planet where the galactic ghost gem was kept.

"I hope Manda is still in one piece," said Regulto. "I trust she made it here."

"No wonder we could never see her again in the first place," said Tiblo.

"Where could she be?" asked Martino.

"Right here!" a voice called behind the others. It was Manda. The rest of the crew turned to her. "Thought you lost me, didn't you."

"You're back!" said Martino.

"I hope those aliens didn't torture you," said Skinamar.

"Just once," said Manda. "But my father was there for me."

CHAPTER 18

DEAD PLANET

As the freedom fighters flew clear across the asteroid field following Brain Tentacles on the same voyage, they found a barren, deserted planet about a light second away. They landed there as the Forbidden UFO hovered past.

"What are we doing here?" asked Martino.

"Looking for clues," said Tiblo. "Everyone get some suits on! There's no oxygen on this planet."

The freedom fighters dressed up in space suits and walked off the Great Red Shark. They traveled on the planet's surface. There was no oxygen to breathe or any surviving life forms. Suddenly, Martino found an alien life form's skeleton. It was long with tail flukes and a long, pointed beak. Martino walked to it.

"Hey, come over here!" he called the others. They went to where he stopped in front of the skeleton.

"This must be a scaled whale," said Tiblo.

"Scaled whale?" Martino asked.

"It's like a scaly skinned, land-dwelling kind of whale," Tiblo explained. "Instead of swimming in water, it slides around on land."

"This planet is a complete wasteland," said Shana. "Look at all the plants on it, they're smoked to a crisp. It looks like it was been on by alien polluters."

"Hey, look!" Skinamar shouted as he spotted a green planet in the sky. "That must be the planet we're seeking."

The Forbidden UFO was slowly approaching that planet.

"Good eye, Skinamar!" said Martino.

"That's it!" said Tiblo. "That's our voyage." He led the others back to the Great Red Shark. They all climbed aboard and took off the spacesuits. Tiblo flew the ship up to where the Forbidden UFO was hovering and then straight to the tropical planet.

"Let those freedom fighters witness their clue for the gem," said Brain Tentacles. "Grick! McGriggle! . . ." he called those two aliens.

"Yes, master," said Grick and McGriggle.

"Fly down to the planet and follow those heroes," Brain Tentacles commanded. "Throw an alarm when they find the gem."

"As you wish," said Grick and McGriggle. They hurried down to the UFO's hangar to fly a pod to the planet's surface.

Meanwhile, the Great Red Shark was landed into an alien tropical jungle. They all searched for clues to the galactic ghost gem, walking off board.

CHAPTER 19

THE GEM IN A CANISTER

"Hey, check this out!" said Martino as he found a giant rock with a message, running to it. The others followed him there. Martino read the message aloud:

"Here lies Mrs. Prunella Solemn Tenderborne, poisoned by a zardnog on this planet while guarding the Phantom of the Galaxy."

"What's a zardnog?" he asked.

"It must be some kind of alien on this planet," said Tiblo.

"Whatever it is, I'm not going for it," said Skinamar.

"Is that really Dr. Brain Tenderborne's wife?" asked Shana.

"If she's been guarding the gem, then . . ." said Martino.

"It must be hidden here somewhere," added Manda. The freedom fighters entered the jungle.

"Still no sign of those aliens," said Tiblo. "We got here first."

"I'm collecting fruit from these trees," said Skinamar. The crew found a fork in the road of two paths.

"This will be perfect time to split up," said Tiblo. "I'm taking the girls this way . . ." He pointed to the right path. ". . . the rest of you go that way." He pointed to the left path. Tiblo, Manda, and Shana walked through the right path as Martino, Skinamar, and Regulto walked through the left.

Meanwhile, Grick and McGriggle landed their pod next to the Great Red Shark. They jumped out and sensed the heroes' scent walking the path far ahead.

"We will encounter them in no time," said McGriggle.

"In no time at all, they're in our hands," said Grick. McGriggle pounded him on the head.

"That's what I'm saying, you idiot," McGriggle said. "Let's go this way." He chose the left path. Grick followed him.

Meanwhile, on the path with Tiblo and the girls, things were about to get a little risky. Manda sniffed around.

"My nose senses danger," she said.

"I hope we're going the right way," said Shana. Tiblo brought out his blasters.

"We might have some alien activity on this planet worse than I expect it," he said.

Suddenly, a hideous small alien showed up, looking like a scorpion with tentacles having poisonous stingers.

"By all gods!" said Tiblo. "That must be a zardnog!" He shot the creature with one of his blasters.

"Good nose," said Shana to Manda.

"All in a day's work," said Manda.

And so, with Martino, Skinamar, and Regulto, they stumbled across a road of dark soil and graphite rocks.

"Stay on high alert," said Martino. "There can be dangers around here."

"I'm collecting the melons up there," said Skinamar as he stretched his arm to a nearby tree branch. He climbed up it and starting packing the melons in his pack.

"Skinamar, wait!" Martino called up to him.

"Just thought I'd increase our food supply," Skinamar replied.

"It can be dangerous all around here," said Martino.

Suddenly, voices sounded around the jungle.

"Yes, I can hear it now," said Regulto.

"Quick, grab my arms!" Skinamar said stretching his arms down to the two humans. He picked them up and set them next to him on the tree branch.

"Way to go, Skinamar," said Martino. The voices came from Grick and McGriggle. They hacked their way through the brush with their bare hands.

"Those heroes should be heard around here by now," said McGriggle.

"I'll bet they show their faces by the ruin," said Grick.

"This way," McGriggle pointed by the tree where the heroes hid above. Grick followed him. Martino used the force in his mind to move the tree's root in his sight. Grick and McGriggle walked by the path and tripped over the root stumbling down.

"Watch your feet, you stupid idiot!" McGriggle shouted to Grick.

"That wasn't me. It was the tree," said Grick.

"Oh yeah, right," said McGriggle. "I forgot how thick these roots were, but . . ." he looked at the root as it moved back to its rightful position. "Okay . . ." he said. "We're good." He and Grick continued their mission.

"Watch this," Skinamar whispered to the others. He grabbed a melon from a nearby branch above and tossed it in the air. Then it fell on McGriggle's head.

"Oof!" he said. "What's the deal?!"

"Whatever it was, it wasn't me," said Grick.

"Let's go ahead and find them," said McGriggle. The two aliens ran ahead to hide in the bushes ahead.

"They're heading for the canister," said Martino. He, Skinamar, and Regulto leaped off the tree back down to the ground.

"We've walked so far and no sign of Tiblo and the girls," said Skinamar.

"There's the ruin!" said Martino pointing ahead.

"We must have the canister in our sights," said Regulto. The three went ahead as Grick and McGriggle watched them in their hiding place.

As Martino, Regulto, and Skinamar reached the ancient ruin, there stood a canister, which contained the galactic ghost gem, on a pedestal in the center of its room.

"That's it!" said Skinamar. "The gem that we're after!"

Suddenly, Tiblo and the girls showed up nearby.

"Marty!" Tiblo said. "Have you seen the gem?"

"Yes, it's in there," said Martino as he pointed inside the ruin.

"Great work, Marty," said Shana.

"My father said we shouldn't break it," said Manda. "Otherwise something mysterious happens from inside it."

"Everything will be fine," said Martino.

"Yeah, we know how to handle jewelry," said Skinamar.

"I should warn you this is very dangerous," said Manda.

"Well, I'm done talking about this," said Martino.

"So am I," said Tiblo.

Grick and McGriggle contacted the other aliens.

"The freedom fighters are at the ruin, master," they said.

"Excellent," said Brain Tentacles. He turned to his minions and said, "Go forth and stop those heroes! And bring me the gem!"

The aliens obeyed his orders. They went down to the hangar bay and boarded space pods with three fitting in each pod at the most. They all flew down to the planet to find the freedom fighters.

Meanwhile, the heroes entered the ruin. Tiblo grabbed the canister and then suddenly, the walls crumbled around them.

"Let's go!" Tiblo shouted. They all ran out of the ruin. The ruin fell into a pile of ancient rocks.

"You actually activated a trap in that ruin," said Martino. Tiblo opened the canister and slid the gem out onto his paw.

"We must keep this safe," he said.

"I'll hold onto it," said Martino grabbing the gem and putting it in his hip pocket. Suddenly, the aliens arrived at the moment.

"Split up!" Tiblo commanded. The freedom fighters scrambled away from the ruin. They left the canister behind. Hizzly showed up and grabbed it. Tiblo went one way as Hizzly flew away with the canister. Tiblo shot one of his wings. Hizzly's snake body fell to the ground.

"Hey, amigo!" he called up to his wings. "Amigo!" The wings lowered down. "Follow my voice!" The arms felt a tree branch and the bat-like body fell. "No," said Hizzly. "That's a tree."

Tiblo and the others continued fighting the aliens. Manda waved her light saber. Shana threw her boomerang around. Regulto defended himself with his bazooka. Some of the aliens grabbed Skinamar, stretching his arms.

"Skinamar, careful!" Martino cried to him.

"Stupid slime balls, let me go!" said Skinamar. The aliens stopped stretching his arms and had them return to their normal length.

"I've had about enough of you, orangutan," said Rumble Bog.

"Skinamar, no!" Martino shouted. "Leave him alone!" he shouted to the aliens. He shot his disk launcher at them. The aliens released Skinamar.

"Thanks a lot, Marty," Skinamar said. "Way to blast them away." Grick and McGriggle came by.

"Take care of them," said McGriggle. "We gotta report to Brain Tentacles."

"Yeah," said Grick. They went back to one of the space pods. They flew back to the UFO. Tiblo grabbed the canister from in front of the ruin and ran quickly among the path back to the Great Red Shark as the others kept fighting the aliens until they were able to break free. They hurried to escape following Tiblo down the path back to the landing site.

"The fight is over!" said Rumble Bog.

"Let's get back to Brain Tentacles," said Cyglimpse. The aliens scrambled back to their pods in the landing zone. Tiblo, on the other hand, started the Great Red Shark's engines and started hovering as the aliens flew back to the Forbidden UFO.

CHAPTER 20

SPACE CHASE

And so, they were all in space lifting off the planet. The Great Red Shark was carried off as the Forbidden UFO followed it behind. The chase was on.

"We have the canister, master," said Rumble Bog to Brain Tentacles.

"Excellent, set it somewhere," said Brain Tentacles. "We'll have to deal with these heroes first."

The Great Red Shark's engines were still at normal pace. Tiblo tried activating the hyper-drive.

"Those aliens can't stand a chance," he said. "Watch this." As he flipped the switch, the power's sound mumbled. Nothing happened.

"Watch what?" asked Manda.

"We have a problem," Tiblo said.

"Talk to Houston about it," said Skinamar.

"We're not going anywhere," said Martino.

"Except to the end of our lives," said Regulto.

"Don't be absurd," said Shana.

Back in the Forbidden UFO, Brain Tentacles gave commands, "Activate our guns!"

"Right away," said McGriggle and Grick.

"We're gonna need some artillery," said Tiblo. Manda, Shana, Regulto, and Martino ran to the ladders that led them to the space guns, two above and two below. The guns on both ships fired back and forth. Tiblo pressed a button on the dashboard that activated the Great Red Shark's shield. Even the UFO had a shield generator, too.

"Let them face the triple missile guns," said Brain Tentacles.

"Yes, master," said Mr. Barfer as he went to the other aliens and said, "Activate the missile launchers." The aliens activated the triple missile launchers that appeared on top of the UFO. They shot three missiles at the same time. Tiblo flew the Shark up and down as fast as he could to avoid the missiles until they exploded. The Great Red Shark vanished afterward.

"We lost them!" said Hizzly, put back together, to Brain Tentacles.

"Don't be afraid," said Brain Tentacles. "They'll be ours later."

The Great Red Shark flew out of sight and then the freedom fighters were alone.

"Way to get us out of that mess," said Martino as he was damaged from the evasion, against his gun's handles. Skinamar was hiding behind the farthest seat row.

"I thought we were alien food," he said, panting. The freedom fighters regrouped together in seats. The Great Red Shark was still out of sight. Suddenly, it flew near a Serpential scale cruiser.

"Target in sight," said a Serpential officer. He activated some of the laser cannons. The Great Red Shark's shield generator ran out of power.

"Great!" said Tiblo. As the cruiser's cannons fired at the Shark, he flew it underneath the ship.

Darth Waternoose approached the officers and said, "Do we have the enemy in our presence?"

"Not exactly," said an officer. "They just fled away."

"I have a better plan," said Waternoose as he walked away. Later in another room in the center of the cruiser, Waternoose found Admiral MacFnurd.

"Admiral!" Waternoose said.

"Yes, Lord Waternoose," the admiral responded.

"Our Heavenly Federal freedom fighters are on the loose," said Waternoose, "but they have nowhere to run. We must set a trap for them. Nala Boomer has been revived by Artidector. Someone could be in good use."

"I'll take care of that," said the admiral. "The trap will be set as soon as I have my men ready."

"Don't fail me again."

"I won't."

"I want that ship in good hands." Waternoose walked out of the room.

Meanwhile, the Great Red Shark had its fins attached at the bottom of the cruiser. The freedom fighters relaxed. The Invisi-Bot scrambled near the dashboard.

"I don't mean to brag," he said. "But this upside-down business is getting me dizzy."

Suddenly, the monitor beeped bringing a new message on the screen. Tiblo looked at it.

"Something says, 'head for planet Maltor'," he read it.

"What's there?" asked Martino.

"A gas planet a few ten miles from here," said Tiblo. "There's a city there with just a few acres of oxygen held there." The monitor beeped again. "Oh, wait!" Tiblo found another message. "Something here says . . ." he read it. ". . . Pangera . . ."

"What is 'Pangera', a nation or something?" asked Manda.

"No, he's a panther that I met before," said Tiblo, "Pangera Pelwoski, my old school friend. We were always gambling, playing classic Earth games, and winning prize money in the lottery. That's where and how I got this ship. Let's get out of here. Detach!" The ship's fins lifted off and the ship turned straight up and it flew away, heading for the gas planet of Maltor.

CHAPTER 21

NALA BOOMER RETURNS

Meanwhile, on Earth's moon, Nala Boomer and Steve Irwin were at the end of training.

"Your training is complete," said Artidector.

"Yes," said Nala.

"Now I'm ready for a new hero's life," said Steve.

"The Force awaits you both," said Artidector. He pointed to several stars and created an imaginary line connecting them to form a constellation.

"Is the Serpent's Ghost really strong?" asked Nala.

"It depends whether you fear it or not," said Artidector."

"I won't let that happen," said Nala.

And so, back in distant space, Brain Tentacles sought that his summoners, the Serpentials, had the freedom fighters under control.

"Those freedom fighters are history," he said. "There is nowhere for them to run now." The aliens carried the canister nearby from when they fought by the ruin.

"Open the canister," Brain Tentacles said to them. "Open the canister, I must see it!"

"Coming up!" said Hizzly as he flew toward him, carrying the canister. He opened it and looked inside. The gem wasn't there.

"It's empty, master," he said.

"What?!?" Brain Tentacles shouted. He grabbed the canister fiercely and growled, "D*** those freedom FIGHTERS!" He spread his arms as he screamed. The Forbidden UFO continued its next voyage for the Heavenly Federal fortress. Brain Tentacles decided to take revenge.

CHAPTER 22

TIBLO'S FRIENDSHIP MAINTENANCE

And so, the freedom fighters entered the atmosphere of Maltor. As Tiblo flew the ship toward the city known as Heloid, a city floating over helium decorated with bowl-shaped skyscrapers, a flying robot followed the Great Red Shark and spoke to Tiblo saying, "You are trespassing on publicity from a different planet. Do you have a permit?"

"No," Tiblo said. "I don't have a landing permit. I'm trying to reach Pangera Pelwoski!"

"Very well," said the robot. "Head for Platform 7."

Tiblo flew the ship into clouds ahead and found Heloid. He looked for Platform 7. He finally found it and landed the ship there. The number 7 was marked in the center circle. After landing the ship, the freedom fighters walked off on the door's conveyor belt.

"There's no one here," said Martino.

"Definitely no one here to see us at all," said the Invisi-Bot following behind.

Suddenly, a door in the nearby tower opened. Out came two alien security guards following a black panther dressed in a red silk robe.

"Scouts," said Tiblo. "Meet my old friend, Pangera Pelwoski." He waved his paw pointing to the panther walking towards them.

"Well, well, well," said Pangera Pelwoski. "Look what the cat dragged in." He finally confronted Tiblo. He raised a paw up and opened it like he was about to scratch Tiblo. But he put his arms around him and laughed, "How are you doing, tiger?! I missed you."

"Yeah, it's been forever," said Tiblo. "I think you should help us around here." He pointed to the Great Red Shark behind him.

"What have you done to my ship?" Pangera asked.

"YOUR ship??" Tiblo asked.

"Yes, MY ship. I bought it first and I let you have it . . ."

"He seems very friendly," said the Invisi-Bot.

"Yes, very friendly," said Manda. The rest of the crew walked toward the two big cats talking.

"Well, let's have a look at your crew," Pangera said to Tiblo. "Who might you be, Mr. Human?" he asked Martino.

"Martino Izodorro," Martino answered.

"And who's your ape partner?" Pangera asked pointing to Skinamar.

"I'm Skinamarinky-Dinky-Dink Skinamarinky-Doo," Skinamar answered.

"And who are you, Miss?" Pangera looked at Manda.

"Manda Monka," she answered.

"And you . . . ?" Pangera looked at Shana.

"Shana Cargon," she answered.

"And who's that guy?" Pangera pointed to Regulto.

"That's Regulto Beauxon," said Tiblo. "He has an alter ego form of a beast. We caught him escaping prison once."

"Really?" said Pangera. "Why don't you all follow me inside for some refreshments?" He walked back toward the tower as the freedom fighters followed him inside. As they did, they walked down a spiral staircase down into the building combined with a lounge, a laboratory, and hotel rooms. The Invisi-Bot headed for the laboratory.

"I wonder if anyone in here can help," he said as the door opened. Another robot came out.

"Move out of the way," it said.

"How rude," said the Invisi-Bot entering the lab. There were aliens working inside. The Invisi-Bot pulled a giant bar-like switch that electrocuted him for ten seconds. The working aliens turned around as they heard the noise. After the seconds, the power zapped a large noise and turned the Invisi-Bot off. Meanwhile, Skinamar noticed the Invisi-Bot was missing.

"Uh," he looked behind himself. "I'll catch up later, our robot is missing." He scampered to the lab back where they started as the rest of the crew entered a lounge room two doors ahead. An alien opened the lab door holding the Invisi-Bot within a folded arm.

"Does anyone own this robot?!" he called out. Skinamar got there just in time as he heard.

"I do, sir," he said. "My group owns it."

"Well, take it," said the alien. "Make sure it stays out of our business!" He set the Invisi-Bot on the solid floor.

"Yes, sir," said Skinamar as he started dragging the Invisi-Bot over to where the others had gone.

Meanwhile, Pangera led the crew in the lounge of rubber sofas and alien plants in large urns.

"Go ahead and make yourselves comfortable," he said. "Here are the refreshments if you want a bite to eat." He showed a counter of refreshments. There happened to be bowls of salads from alien fruits and vegetables, and bites of bacon from foreign beasts. The freedom fighters set themselves on the furniture.

I wonder what these strangers have to do with the Great Red Shark, thought Martino. "Has anyone seen Skinamar and the Invisi-Bot?" he asked out loud.

"Coming in!" Skinamar called out as he dragged the shut off Invisi-Bot in the lounge. The freedom fighters stood up and confronted Skinamar.

"I wondered where you were," said Pangera.

"I kind of got lost behind the rest of you with the Invisi-Bot here," Skinamar explained.

"Is that the Invisi-Bot?" asked Tiblo. "What happened to him?"

"He was electrocuted in an alien laboratory and the whole thing shut him off," said Skinamar.

"Oh no," said Manda. "Skinamar, do you think you can fix him?"

"I'll try," Skinamar got to work, taking the Invisi-Bot apart finding out if any wires were jammed that prevented the Invisi-Bot from working.

"I'll help you out," said Shana going to Skinamar with the wires and cables.

"Bedrooms are for rent if you guys get sleepy," Pangera announced.

"Thanks," said Tiblo.

And so, the freedom fighters enjoyed their stay in the hotel, unaware of what might happen badly the next day. The situation is yet to involve the Serpential forces. But the truth was about to come clear.

CHAPTER 23

THE FUTURE

So it passed; on the moon, thoughts arose in Nala Boomer's head about the danger with the freedom fighters. Zinger Warsp was there.

"Friends will be in need to save," said Zinger as he hovered.

"The freedom fighters," Nala said to herself.

"I'm aware of that," said Steve.

"Since training is complete," said Zinger, "you can go, so be careful." Artidector appeared nearby.

"It is dangerous as you are involved," he said.

"I'm aware," said Nala.

"Listen to Artidector," said Zinger to Nala and Steve.

"I not want to lose you again, Nala Boomer," said Artidector.

"You won't," said Nala. "I promise I'll return to you."

"It is the future you feel," said Zinger. "They might die unless you help them."

"That's exactly what I'm doing," said Nala.

"I've never been a freedom fighter before," said Steve.

"Nala," said Artidector. "Give not into fear of evil. That leads to the Serpent's Ghost." Nala and Steve got into their new spaceships that Artidector constructed like models.

"We will return," said Nala. "We promise." She and Steve flew away into space.

"She is one living legend we brought back from the dead," said Zinger.

"That lioness is our last and only hope," said Artidector.

"No," said Zinger. "There are many others . . . with pure of heart."

Nala and Steve flew out into space. They followed the Force in search for the real freedom fighters.

CHAPTER 24

A TRAP

And so, the six real freedom fighters woke up the next morning in Heloid. Strange feelings arose within them as they lounged on the sofas.

"So when are we gonna get the hyper-drive repaired?" asked Martino.

"I don't know yet," said Tiblo. "But we must take care of business right now."

"We just have to be patient," said Skinamar as he helped repair the Invisi-Bot.

"How's he coming?" Martino asked as Skinamar, Shana, and Regulto repaired the robot.

"His wires seemed to be jammed really bad," said Shana. "We'll get them straight in no time."

"His power must be low," said Regulto.

"Leave that to me," said Skinamar.

Manda approached and confronted Tiblo.

"I don't feel comfortable here," she said. "This seems to have no help with the hyper-driving system."

"Now that we're here, we must follow Pangera's instructions whatever he tells us," Tiblo explained.

"I don't trust Pangera!" said Manda.

"Well, I don't trust him either," said Tiblo. "But we don't have a choice . . . ." He rested his paws on Manda's shoulders. "He's still my friend."

Pangera arrived in the lounge room and flung his paw toward his face saying, "All right, follow me, heroes, we're about to meet somebody." The freedom fighters followed him.

"I hope it's nobody we know who is bad," said Tiblo.

As they all walked to a nearby conference room, Pangera opened the doors with a button on the wall next to them. Inside appeared Darth Waternoose, who stood up on the other side of the table. Tiblo fetched out one of his blasters and tried shooting at Waternoose repeatedly as Waternoose blocked the shots with his hand. He used the Force to pull Tiblo's blaster all the way toward himself. He caught it in his hand.

"Your wide-eyed adventures have gone far enough, freedom fighters," he said. Scale troopers surrounded the freedom fighters outside the room carrying blasters in their hands.

"I was told to bring you to your enemies, because I had no choice," said Pangera. "I'm sorry."

"Well, I'm sorry, too," said Tiblo. Scale troopers grabbed him and carried him to nearby room. Inside was a table with electric wires and spires that looked like dental drills. The troopers placed Tiblo on the bed and grabbed some spires and poked them on Tiblo's body. It was a torture room. A nearby lizard turned on a large power generator, throwing the switch up. The spires placed on Tiblo electrocuted him.

"Augh! Oh-augh! OW!" he screamed out loud as the others heard him.

Skinamar was finished putting the Invisi-Bot back together. Scale troopers led the remaining freedom fighters to a nearby prison cell.

"Have a seat," one of the troopers ordered. They closed the door as the freedom fighters sat on benches or beds.

"What are they doing to us?" asked Martino.

"Whatever it is, it must be a trick," said Manda. "And they're playing it on us right now."

Skinamar turned the Invisi-Bot on. He started to reactivate properly. Then he awoke.

"Oh, gracious me! Where are we? What happened?" he started asking.

"It's a long story," said Skinamar. "Just be patient."

"The last thing I remember was entering a laboratory and being electrocuted," said the Invisi-Bot.

"Someone's coming," said Regulto as he heard another scale trooper coming. Regulto backed away as the trooper opened the door carrying Tiblo in the cell and setting him on a bed.

"I feel terrible," Tiblo whimpered as he lay rested.

"This is an imprisonment," said Martino. "We'll never get out of here."

"There must be a way," said Shana. "They're up to no good for the moment."

Outside spoke a scale trooper and Waternoose.

"The prisoners are all in hand," said the trooper.

"Prepare the crystalline chamber," said Waternoose.

"Yes, sir," said the trooper as he walked away.

Inside the cell, Manda put her arm on Tiblo and asked, "Why are they doing this?"

"I don't know," said Tiblo.

"Maybe it's because they hate us," said Skinamar.

And so, Darth Waternoose and the scale troopers activated a chamber with melting crystals in tanks of glass. Aliens collected different gems from many different worlds. Darth Waternoose walked back into the hall and told an officer to prepare a welcome for Nala Boomer.

"Right away, my lord," said the officer, as he headed for a nearby landing zone.

Meanwhile, Pangera returned to confront Waternoose.

"Mr. Pelwoski, your friends shall have to face a special fate," Waternoose said.

"I saved your pity, Lord Waternoose," said Pangera. "My friends can't survive under your clutches."

"I'll have them unharmed," said Waternoose.

"I shall have my promises for Captain Tigro in my hands," said Pangera.

"Perhaps, you think you're being treated unfairly."

"No." Pangera walked away to the freedom fighters' cell. He opened the door and marched inside. Tiblo quickly jumped off the bed after resting from the electrical numbness and said, "Get out of our lives, Pangera . . . !"

"Shut up and listen!" Pangera quickly snapped back. "Waternoose has planned your destination."

"And where would he want us?" asked Martino.

"You really are getting us eliminated, especially your own friends, Pangy!" said Skinamar.

"The trap will be set if you all listen and trust me around here," said Pangera.

"Waternoose wants us all dead, doesn't he," said Manda.

"He doesn't want you at all," said Pangera, "he's after somebody called, um . . . Boomer."

"You mean *Nala* Boomer?" asked Skinamar.

"The lioness?" asked Martino.

"That's what they all said," said Pangera. "A trap is set."

"And we're the bait!" said Manda.

"Exactly," said Pangera. "Now, everyone follow me." He led the freedom fighters out of the cell. Skinamar finally had the Invisi-Bot standing on his feet once again. They both joined the others out in the hall. Pangera closed the door with the button that made them slide shut.

Meanwhile, Nala Boomer landed her new ship on a nearby zone's platform, then so did Steve Irwin.

"I'm going alone," said Nala. "Someone is expecting me."

"As you wish," said Steve. "I think I'll find the others." Nala entered the building. Steve went into another door around it.

Inside the building, Pangera led the freedom fighters into a wide room with two floors made of metal crossbars forming rectangular holes within.

"What an open source," said Martino. The Serpentials waited for the heroes in the middle of the room where there was steam hissing out of pipes. Officers, along with Darth Waternoose, Count Joustiáño, and Carpoon, were there.

"What's happening here?" asked Tiblo.

"You're about to be put into crystal-freeze," Pangera answered. He and the crew approached the Serpentials standing around a circle in the middle of the level.

"Bring them forward, Pelwoski," said Joustiáño. Pangera followed the command and he and the heroes approached the center.

"Crystal-freeze power generator is ready," said an alien from below.

"Good luck, scouts," said Tiblo as he started stepping forward.

"No, Captain, don't do this!" shouted Regulto.

"Tiblo," said Manda as Tiblo stopped. "I won't let you leave me."

"Very uneager creatures we have," said Carpoon.

"This is suicide!" shouted Skinamar.

"Tiblo, please," said Manda.

"Manda, look at me," Tiblo said. "I did promise long ago that I wouldn't leave you alone in danger . . ." He remembered a time when he first trained Manda in the academy as a scout to a leader. ". . . but I now have to break that promise." He walked to the circle and stood there.

"I love you," said Manda.

"I know," said Tiblo, "as if I were a father to you." The circle lowered and steam flowed below. Tiblo was placed within a vertical bed in which he was locked in binds by his paws. Steam was emerging and Tiblo closed his eyes after seeing a hot gelatin substance that covered him and cooled off with Tiblo inside a giant gem. The process was complete. The gem rose with metal bars protecting it from breaking. The freedom fighters were in shock of their captain.

"By the way," said Carpoon. "Lord Waternoose said you had a gem with you."

"Right here," said Martino as he grabbed a bag with the galactic ghost gem inside. He tossed it over to Carpoon who caught it.

"I'll take care of your captain," he said. He took off with scale troopers carrying Tiblo sealed in the giant crystal.

Darth Waternoose turned to Count Joustiáño and said, "Take the others to the lobby."

"Bind them," Joustiáño commanded the scale troopers. They used brass binders for each freedom fighter's hands behind his or her back, except for Skinamar, scale troopers tried to grab him as he fled the trap, stretching his arms up to a nearby vent that led to an airway.

"You guys are on your own, now!" he called down to the others.

"That orangutan just got away," said one of the troopers.

"Forget the ape!" said Joustiáño. "Gag them." The scale troopers brought out small cloths of silk or rubber and used them as gags for the heroes' mouths. They tied them on the back of their heads. The troopers led the freedom fighters to the lobby. Pangera followed them. Darth Waternoose looked down at the aliens below and said, "Reset the chamber for Nala Boomer." The aliens followed his request.

And so, Boomer had arrived with her new ship landed on a nearby tarmac plate along with Steve Irwin's ship.

CHAPTER 25

FREEDOM FIGHTER HOSTAGE

Moments grew about. Nala Boomer and Steve Irwin went two different directions. Skinamar saw them both outside a window vent as he snuck through the airway.

"I must face Waternoose," said Nala.

"I'll find the other heroes," said Steve.

Skinamar slid down a slope in the airway and tried to follow the freedom fighters being taken to the lobby. As Nala walked inside the hall, arming herself with her blaster held up, she found the freedom fighters bound walking with the scale troopers and Serpential officers. The Invisi-Bot was locked in a cage with wheels. Nala witnessed them all as Manda saw her. She could not speak clear because of the gag in her mouth. Nala continued moving through the hallway.

And so, the freedom fighters were taken in the lobby and the troopers set them on a round rubber couch. Count Joustiáño turned on a communication system on a dome-shaped table. He contacted the emperor, Hieronymus Sharp.

"My liege," said Joustiáño, "we have the heroes here."

"Excellent," the emperor hissed with his forked tongue. "Remove the gags." The scale troopers took the gags off of the freedom fighters so they would have a right to speak.

"Emperor Sharp," said Martino. "You were always a winner in war, especially when you defeated my parents."

"How typical for you to remember, Martino Izodorro," said the emperor. "Your sister remains alive in that ice crystal unable to breathe for years."

"You only had *my* sister die but Artidector saved me," said Manda.

"And it's your fault the chief of my herd banished me," said Shana.

The emperor laughed. "Interesting accusations," he said, "but there will be no possibility for you freedom fighters to win the rest of this war."

Skinamar peeked through a vent above the room and saw the freedom fighters talking to the emperor on the communication system. The emperor's hologram vanished as he flicked his forked tongue. Skinamar looked around the airway in other vents for more clues.

CHAPTER 26

BOOMER VERSUS WATERNOOSE

Meanwhile, Nala Boomer walked into the same door where the freedom fighters were led into, entering the crystal-freeze chamber. She stood on one foot and held her blaster in front of her face and looked around for Darth Waternoose, according to her destiny. She snuck toward the center circle of the chamber.

"The Force is with you, Nala," Waternoose's voice emerged from across the center from where Nala walked. "But you are not the freedom fighter you once were." He appeared upstairs from where Nala stopped as she found him. Waternoose lit his light saber and Nala turned on her blaster. She walked up the stairs as they both approached each other. The fight went on. They descended the staircase; Waternoose herded Nala to the center circle of the chamber.

"Your journey to the emperor begins here," Waternoose scolded. The circle opened. Nala fell into the hole. The aliens activated the system. The bed approached her and steam emerged among her. Suddenly, she escaped by jumping off a wall from the hole and leaped out for her life. Waternoose approached the hole as it steamed like a geyser. He found Nala hanging on a steam pipe above the hole.

"Impressive," said Waternoose.

Nala fell back to the floor and continued the fight with Waternoose. Waternoose stepped back as he waved his light saber around blocking off Nala's blaster shots as she used it.

"OUGH!" Waternoose shouted as he fell to a lower level. Nala stopped firing and looked where Waternoose fell. Below was dark and pitch black. A burning thrust sound occurred. Waternoose flew up with his rocket engine attached to his back.

"Come below," he said to Nala as he drove back down to the lower level. Nala followed him and leaped down to the next floor, searching for where Waternoose hid. She landed on her paws as if she were exercising with a push-up. She stood back up and searched for Waternoose in the darkness.

CHAPTER 27

SKINAMAR'S SECRET

The four remaining freedom fighters sat in the lobby with their hands bound and pirate knights guarding the entrance. Suddenly, Martino came up with a bright idea. He scooted near Regulto and said, "I got a plan."

"What?" Regulto asked.

"Can you reach my hip pocket?" Martino asked back. Regulto turned himself around and inserted his hands still bound into Martino's pocket.

"What am I looking for?" he asked.

"My lucky charm," said Martino. "A laser torch."

Shana turned her head to the two humans.

"What are you two doing?" she asked.

"I'm trying to get us out of here," said Martino. Regulto activated the laser torch and tried to focus with his head turned around, burning the binders on Martino's wrists. The torch's beam melted the brass. After that, Martino's hands were free.

Meanwhile, a thud slammed against the air vent above. Skinamar was breaking out. He held onto the bars and stretched his arms, moving his body back like a slingshot. He launched his body and broke through the vent and fell into the lobby.

"Skinamar!" Martino said in surprise.

"How's it hanging, guys?" Skinamar asked.

"Where have you been?" said the Invisi-Bot still in the cage with wheels. "You're with us again at last!"

Martino and Skinamar unlocked the binders on the other freedom fighters' hands.

"I have a secret, everyone," Skinamar spoke. "The bounty hunter hasn't left yet. He still has the captain near his ship." He grabbed the handled rod that pulled the cage with the Invisi-Bot inside. The others opened the doors and the pirate knights guarding them turned around and activated their weapons. The freedom fighters fought against them. As they did, Regulto drank his medicine. He threw the flask out of sight and it broke on faraway floor. As he waited for it to work, he fired his bazooka and blasted the pirate knights away. They were later tired. The hallway was nearly wreckage.

"Hurry!" said the Invisi-Bot. "We must save Tiblo Tigro from the bounty hunter!" Skinamar pulled the cage that held him.

"This way, guys," Skinamar called to the others. They all ran through the hallway to find Carpoon's ship on an outside tarmac as Regulto started to develop into Rufus the beast.

Meanwhile at that tarmac, Carpoon was getting ready for takeoff in his ship. Scale troopers loaded Tiblo frozen in a crystal aboard. Carpoon jumped into the cockpit. The troopers left the area. The freedom fighters arrived on a bridge that led to the tarmac as Carpoon started his ship and began to fly away.

"We're too late!" said Martino.

"Plan B, guys," said Skinamar. "I have some more secrets. Pangera Pelwoski is done working with the enemy right now. Nala Boomer is fighting against Waternoose, perhaps she's in his clutches. And Steve Irwin is trying to join us. Follow me!" The freedom fighters all ran back into the building. Rufus was fully developed from Regulto's medicine. Inside the smoldering hallway, Steve Irwin was still looking for the freedom fighters. Pangera sat in the lobby. The pirate knights were hopefully gone, perhaps marching back to their fleet ships.

Meanwhile, Nala Boomer was still looking for Waternoose still hiding in the darkness of the hallway below. She moved near a column. Suddenly, a robotic tentacle grasped it. It was Waternoose. He lit his light saber again and Nala continued firing her blaster. They moved near a large round window. Waternoose used the force to grab a power box from a wall across from the window. He moved it around Nala. She dodged it and then kicked it at the window. It broke it open and a vacuum-like force sucked Nala out into the open air. Waternoose turned himself around as he was being pulled out, too.

And so, after the freedom fighters met up with Steve Irwin in the hallway, Skinamar led the crew into the lobby where Pangera sat on the circular couch.

"Skinamar was right," said Martino. "He *has* stopped working with the other side."

"Just go to him, Marty," said Skinamar. "Just ask him if he can help us escape."

"I don't like this," said Shana.

"Okay, I'll talk to him," said Martino.

"But, Martino," said Manda, "he's one of them."

"Well, he's one of *us,* now," said Martino. He walked toward Pangera and started speaking, "Hey, Pangera, can you help us escape?"

Pangera sighed and said, "I saved their pity. I have been imprisoned to do their bidding. Now I can *so* help you escape, since Tiblo is out of here."

"Alright," said Martino. "Let's get going." As he and Pangera walked out of the lobby, Rufus frowned as he looked at Pangera.

"You should be punished," Rufus growled as he grabbed Pangera's neck with both hands trying to choke him.

"Rufus, NO!" shouted Martino.

"Oh boy," said Skinamar.

"What do you have to say for yourself abandoning your tiger friend?" Rufus asked Pangera.

"It . . . <cack> . . . doesn't matter," Pangera tried speaking as he was being choked.

"What do you think you're doing, Rufus?" said the Invisi-Bot. "Trust him! Trust him!"

"You left us no choice, Pangera," said Manda.

"I was . . . <ack> . . . just trying to . . . help," said Pangera.

"Well you did your best," said Manda. "But it failed."

Rufus kept choking Pangera.

"Let him go!" Martino shouted. "You'll kill him!"

"For goodness sake, release the panther!" said the Invisi-Bot. Rufus let Pangera go. He was finally gasping and getting his breath back.

"Finally," said Skinamar.

"I'm terribly sorry about all this," said the Invisi-Bot to Pangera. "After all, he's only a myth."

Pangera got up as the freedom fighters continued through the hallway. Skinamar still dragged the wheeled cage with the Invisi-Bot. Pangera followed everyone. Suddenly, a band of scale troopers patrolled the hallway. They all aimed their blasters at the heroes. The heroes activated their weapons. The troopers fired as the heroes scrambled everywhere. Manda used her light saber to block off blaster shots. Shana used her boomerang to knock or chase away some troopers. Many of them fell to the floor. Skinamar fired his sunray phaser among the troopers. They ran away and the blast melted a hole in the wall ahead. It showed the Great Red Shark outside still sitting where the freedom fighters landed it.

"There's our ship in one piece," said Skinamar. "We're saved!"

"Oh, joy rapture!" said the Invisi-Bot.

"Let me get you out," said Skinamar as he pointed his phaser at the side of the wheeled cage's door. "Better stand back." The Invisi-Bot stood back as Skinamar fired the phaser and moved it up to melt the cage's bars. Soon they were shortened to a crisp.

"I'm free at last!" the Invisi-Bot shouted with glee and walked out but fell apart to the floor with one leg and one arm off. "I'm broken again, how typical."

"Hurry up, guys!" said Martino as the heroes moved ahead to the exit door to the tower nearest to the Great Red Shark.

"Let me get you something, Vizzy," said Skinamar as he went to a nearby wall and opened the hatch on it. Inside was a rubber wire net basket. He pulled it out and carried the Invisi-Bot and his broken-off limbs and set them into the basket.

"Are you sure this basket is necessary?" the Invisi-Bot asked.

"Believe me, it's all I can find," said Skinamar. "Come on, let's go!" He started pushing the basket ahead to where the heroes headed for the exit.

"Serpential ships are everywhere," said Pangera. "They're searching the entire city for fugitives."

"Including *us?*" asked Martino.

"I'm afraid so," said Pangera.

"We better get out of here fast," said Shana. Rufus tried to budge open the exit door, but he was already done with his medicine he turned back into Regulto.

"It's no use," he said.

"Allow me," said Pangera as he pressed a red security button nearby and spoke into the microphone where his voice went through many loudspeakers around the city:

"Attention, civilians. This is Pangera Pelwoski. You all must evacuate this city to avoid the Serpential forces. They are about to conquer it."

The people in the city searched for landing sites with ships. The freedom fighters headed out the door and ran to the Great Red Shark.

"Finally, we're out of here," said Skinamar as he pushed the basket with the Invisi-Bot up the stepping ramp to the entrance door of the ship. Everyone was aboard the Shark. Shana, Regulto, and Skinamar activated the cockpit.

"Crikey!" said Steve Irwin. "What a large spaceship you all have."

The Great Red Shark was flown off the tarmac. But there was one thing they forgot about . . . Nala Boomer.

CHAPTER 28

BACK TO THE TEAM

Meanwhile, the fight between Nala Boomer and Darth Waternoose continued. They climbed up a ladder on a powerhouse, shaped like a trapezoid. Nala went up to the top near the house's door as Waternoose used his jet fire gadget from within his back. As he landed he waved his light saber in front of himself as Nala kept firing her blaster. Waternoose lured her across a bridge that led to the center of the wide open shaft inside the building. In the center was a sensory antenna for generating power. Waternoose fiercely wielded his saber and fended off the blaster shots. Nala fell to the floor. Waternoose pointed his saber in front of her.

"You are beaten," he said. "Now you must surrender."

"Never," said Nala as she scooted back and tried firing her blaster again. Waternoose fended off the shot, which backed off and knocked Nala's blaster away. He quickly lunged and used his saber to burn a wound between Nala's thorax and abdomen. Nala screamed in vain and fell back on the bridge's floor. Waternoose breathed through his machine as Nala scooted toward the antenna.

"Now this is your last chance," said Waternoose. "Do not make me destroy you." He turned off his light saber. Nala tried catching her breath as she approached the antenna.

Waternoose explained, "Join me, and together we can dethrone the emperor. We will end this war between the Sharp Empire and the Heaven Federation, and you can be the last bystander."

"I'll never join you!" Nala shouted as she put her paw on the wound Waternoose gave her.

"If you only knew the power of the Serpent's Ghost," said Waternoose, "Artidector never told you what happened to a dead body once buried in the state of Hawaii back on your home planet."

"He told me enough," said Nala as she clutched on a ring surrounding the antenna. "He said that your soldiers devoured it."

"No," said Waternoose. "Whatever you heard was a lie." Nala started shivering as she listened to Waternoose as he said, "I . . . am that body inside."

"No," said Nala. "It's not true. That's impossible!"

"Look into my eyes," said Waternoose. "You will see the truth . . ." He played holograms like a video projector from his top three eyes, showing the history with pirate knights digging a grave and possessing the dead body. The emperor was shown bringing the body to life in a crablike robot (Waternoose). The future was then displayed with the emperor laughing for his victory in the war. Nala began to weep as she watched the holograms.

"Ugh! NO!" she whimpered out loud.

"Come with me," said Waternoose, "and I will complete your new life. We can rule the galaxy, only me, an overlord, and you, a stewardess."

Nala looked down below where there was a large hole at the bottom with tunnels leading to the bottom of the city. Her eyes watered with tears making her vision blur. Illusions of snake- and worm-like monsters appeared in the tunnels. Nala looked back at Waternoose.

"Come with me," he said. "It is the only way."

Nala panicked and let go of the antenna's outer ring and fell down to one of the tunnels below.

"Foolish lioness," said Waternoose as he watched Nala fall.

She fell into a tunnel and slid through it. It led to the bottom. It was round like a playground's tube slide. She ended up on a hatch that opened under and she fell out into an open air mass below the city. She grabbed a spire that pointed down to an endless free-falling way. She looked down and found her lost blaster falling forever to the planet's core. She climbed up and tried to grab onto one of the hatch's doors, but they already closed up. Soon she was stranded on the spire for a while. There was barely enough oxygen to breathe from any plantation from the city above. The planet was all formed up of gases such as hydrogen and helium.

"Artidector," she spoke weakly. "Zinger, please." She had to use the Force to contact help. It led to the freedom fighters. "Freedom . . . fighters . . . anyone."

As the freedom fighters, along with Steve Irwin and Pangera Pelwoski, flew the Great Red Shark away through the gaseous air, Nala's voice came inside the freedom fighters' heads.

"Boomer," Martino whispered to himself.

"Boomer," Manda whispered the same thing. "We have to go back," she said out loud to the others.

"What??" asked Pangera.

"I figured out where Nala Boomer is," said Manda.

"I was wondering," said Martino.

They turned the ship in a U-turn back to Heloid. It took two minutes to fly back there. The heroes finally approached the city's underside. Pangera pointed out a figure on a spire ahead.

"Look, somebody's up there," he said.

"It's Boomer," said Martino and Manda simultaneously.

"Skinamar, slow down," said Manda. "Slow down."

"I'm trying to," said Skinamar as he moved the steering handles slowly. "Easy now . . . almost there . . . that should do it."

"Shana, can you open the top emergency hatch," Manda said.

"Yep, I got it," Shana said as she pulled a switch that opened a hatch at the ship's ceiling.

"I'll get her," said Pangera as he walked on an elevating platform where he was moved up and out of the ship, reaching Nala Boomer. "Come down," Pangera said to her. Nala climbed down to him. "That's it," he spoke. "Easy." He spread his arms out as Nala fell slowly into them. "There you go." The others waited.

"Pangera?" said Manda.

"Okay, let's go," said Pangera. The platform lowered as he held Nala in his arms. Shana closed the hatch. The heroes were all ready to go. They flew away from the city again and headed for the atmosphere. Minutes later, they were off of the planet Maltor.

Meanwhile, the Forbidden UFO was hovering in space near Maltor. Brain Tentacles watched the Great Red Shark enter space.

"Those intrepid heroes are taken care of by our summoners," he said.

Meanwhile, back in Heloid, Waternoose and the Serpential officers approached any nearest tarmac about to head for space.

"So your fight with Boomer was a failure, my lord," said Admiral Marwick MacFnurd.

"It won't be long until I finally have her in my hands before the emperor," said Waternoose. The Serpentials boarded their ships and headed out for space.

And so, in the Forbidden UFO, Brain Tentacles explained to all of his minions, "The freedom fighters are in our friends' hands by now. I hope we have the galactic ghost gem. Who has the canister?"

Grick and McGriggle walked forward to Brain Tentacles as they held the canister that had held the gem.

"I hate to say this, master," said Grick, "but . . ."

"Open the canister, I must see it," Brain Tentacles commanded. McGriggle unscrewed the canister's lid.

"Here," he said as he gave it to him.

Brain Tentacles grabbed the canister with his crustacean claw and found that it was empty.

"Where is the gem?!" he growled.

"Like I tried to tell you, master," said Grick. "The freedom fighters have taken it."

Brain Tentacles slammed his claw on a nearby metal table. He shouted, "Blast those freedom . . ." He faced the ceiling and spread his arms out. ". . . FIIIIGGGHHHHTEEEERRRRRSS!"

And so, the Great Red Shark flew near a fleet of Serpential ships.

"Scale destroyer," said Manda.

"Do we have the hyper-drive reactivated?" asked Martino.

"It's fixed, but I didn't turn it on yet," said Shana.

Meanwhile, Skinamar was fixing the Invisi-Bot and Nala Boomer was on a bed, resting from her fight with Waternoose. Pangera steered the ship around the scale destroyer. Waternoose was inside that ship.

"Our enemies are surrounding us, my lord," said a Serpential officer.

Waternoose looked at the Great Red Shark and said, "Nala."

"Whoever," said Nala as she heard Waternoose's voice with the Force.

"Friend," said Waternoose, "come with me."

"Artidector," said Nala, "why didn't you tell me." She suddenly screamed in agony about the wound on her front. The heroes heard her.

"I'll go check on her," said Manda. Martino followed her. They went to the back where Nala lay on the emergency bed.

"This wound is from Darth Waternoose's saber," she said.

"You're okay," said Manda. "Just relax." She set her arm over Nala.

"We better get her to a hospital ship," said Martino.

"We will eventually," said Manda. "I'll talk to Pangera about it." She and Martino went back to the cockpit. Nala was barely able to get up from the bed. She used a damp cloth to catch the blood from her wound. She walked slowly between the seat aisles of the upper deck.

"Nala," said Waternoose talking to her with the Force, "it is your destiny."

Nala whimpered again, "Arti . . . dector . . ."

"We better activate the hyper-drive," said Pangera as he moved his paw over the button for the hyper-drive.

Meanwhile, Skinamar went to the hyper-drive's activation system.

"Skinamar, where are you going?" said the Invisi-Bot. "You're not finished repairing me, yet."

"I'm going to activate the hyper-drive," said Skinamar.

"What?!" the Invisi-Bot said aloud. "You don't need to activate the hyper-drive. Miss Cargon can do it."

Skinamar pulled the switch and a humming sound happened. He used a screwdriver to tighten a bolt that twirled a wire like a spaghetti string. He was shocked for a second. "Augh!" he screamed. The hyper-drive was activated. The Great Red Shark zoomed into distant space. Skinamar flipped back and slammed himself on a wall.

"Now that's more like it," said Pangera.

"You did it, Skinamar!" said the Invisi-Bot.

"We lost them," said one of the Serpentials.

"They will be dealt with someday," said Waternoose. "But Boomer is mine to handle."

CHAPTER 29

BOOMER'S HOSPITALITY

Soon, the heroes rejoined the Heaven Federation within their swarm of ships and fortresses. The Great Red Shark was landed in a hangar bay under the hospital ship. They took Nala Boomer up to the right level with beds and curtains. Robotic surgeons scrambled and took care of business. The heroes set Nala on one bed.

"This lioness has a deep wound between her chest and stomach," Manda explained to the surgeon next to the bed.

"I will take a look," said the surgeon as it inched closer to the bed with a wheel for moving around. It found Nala's blood being shed at a nearly large amount. It used a damp cloth from the cupboard next to the bed to absorb the blood. The surgeon used a rubber sensor finger from its left hand to feel how deep the wound was.

As the heroes waited, Martino played his lyre (a gift from Zinger when he first joined the hero team). Pangera walked around the lounge area as the rest of the heroes sat on the rubber couches. The surgeon approached the heroes and said, "The wound is about an inch deep. Her muscle layer is about as thin as Swiss cheese."

"Man," said Martino.

"Good god," said Skinamar, "what a bad, sore cut."

The surgeon returned to Nala and activated a sewing needle gadget with dark, hard thread about to sew a stitch in the wound. It first set a sponge on it to absorb the last amount of blood. It took about three minutes to heal and for the blood to clot.

Martino approached the surgeon and asked, "How long are you working on her?"

"This will take a while," said the surgeon. As it started stitching Nala's wound, Skinamar activated a nearby system that looked like a jukebox, turning to a song entitled "Foolish Heart". The music started as he was ready to sing it:

"I need a love that grows I don't want it unless I know
With each passing hour someone somehow will be there
ready to share
I need a love that's strong . . ."

"Why is he singing with that radio in public?" asked Pangera.

". . . I'm so tired of being alone . . ."

"I don't know, he's just Skinamar," said Martino.

*". . . But will my lonely heart play the part of the fool
again before I begin*

*Foolish heart hear me calling stop before you start falling
Foolish heart heed my warning you've been wrong before
Don't be wrong anymore . . ."*

As the song went on, the surgeon was nearly done stitching Nala's wound.

"A few knots here," it said, "looping around, that should do it."

"Ow!" Nala said as she felt the tight stitch.

"Well," said the surgeon, "that's taken care of."

Skinamar started singing the second verse of the song:

*"Feeling that feeling again I'm playing a game I can't win
Love's knocking on the door of my heart once more
Think I'll let her in before I begin . . ."*

He sang the chorus as the surgeon started explaining, "The wound must heal for at an hour. She will start walking eventually. So just let her rest."

"Right," said Martino.

"Yeah," said Manda and Shana.

Meanwhile, a pod arrived in the hospital ship's hangar bay. It was Zinger. He flew out of his pod and up to where the freedom fighters were.

"Zinger?" Martino said as he noticed him flying by. Zinger fluttered near the heroes and said, "There is much to be told . . . about the galactic ghost gem and Captain Tigro . . ."

As Zinger told the story, Count Joustiáño and Carpoon flew to the planet, Treetop, the farthest planet that followed the Death Scale. They landed their ships near a flesh-colored stone-built palace. Carpoon took out Tiblo Tigro frozen in a crystal as Joustiáño helped drag him inside the palace. Inside sat on a throne a large, tubby monster called King Owpi, who looked like a cross between an owl and a pig with four chubby arms and a thick tail that he used for bouncing around. He would not use his legs very often. Suddenly, a flying reptilian messenger figure flew to Owpi and said, "Your highness, you have visitors." The palace's large door lifted up and Joustiáño and Carpoon entered it. They carried the crystal with Tiblo inside.

"We have things from our officers for you to watch, King Owpi," said Joustiáño.

"Whatever could they be?" asked Owpi.

"Here we have Captain Tiblo Tigro of the Heaven Federation," said Carpoon. "There must be a place for him to stay."

"I'll keep in touch with him," said Owpi.

"And I have this," said Joustiáño as he reached into a pouch hooked onto his belt taking out the gem. He held it in his hand showing it to Owpi and said, "The galactic ghost gem."

"How delicately interesting," said Owpi. He grabbed the gem from Joustiáño's hand and looked at it closely. The phantom inside appeared and said, "Dessstroy . . . desssstroy . . ."

"I will keep in touch with these items," said Owpi.

"Excellent," said Joustiáño. "We shall return to our forces."

"Yes, Count," said Carpoon. The two beasts left the palace. They climbed back into their ships and flew away.

CHAPTER 30

A NEW TEAM

Zinger finished his story and then explained, "Now the Death Scale is put back together. And we will search for Captain Tigro soon enough."

"I'll go look for him," said Pangera. "Any volunteers?"

"I'll come," said Regulto.

"Me, too," said Shana.

"I'm staying," said Skinamar.

"I am, too," said Martino.

"So am I," said Manda.

"We'll take care of Nala here," said Skinamar.

"I'll come," said Steve Irwin. "My space adventures were just beginning."

"Alright," said Pangera. "To the Great Red Shark." He and those who decided to go with him walked down to the hangar bay and climbed aboard the Great Red Shark. Zinger led their way through space, knowing where

Tiblo was being kept. The ship was then flown out of the hospital ship's hangar bay. The rest of the heroes stayed behind and took care of Nala Boomer as her wound healed and she was later able to get up and walk.

And so, the new hero team was settled with five of the true freedom fighters, along with Nala Boomer, Steve Irwin, and Pangera Pelwoski. The later purposes are to get Tiblo Tigro back and to fight the Serpential forces, now that the Death Scale has been rebuilt.

REFERENCE:

Song: "Foolish Heart" by Steve Perry found in Chapter 29